MW00893612

Reviews of *Zombie Turkeys,* Volume 1 of Life After Life Chronicles:

"This book will not only make you laugh out loud, you will be surprised at the tender moments! You'll fly right through it and want more. Mr. Zach has a sense of humor we all need!"- Goodreads

"The yarn is fast-moving from start to finish, opening with the first attack of carnivorous red-eyed wild turkeys very difficult to kill. They can quickly resurrect after death and grow back cut-off limbs. They're led by a tom full of confidence as Zach gives us this tom's perspectives from time to time as he builds his flock into the tens of thousands throughout Illinois and beyond." - Author Dr. Wesley Britton, BookPleasures.com

"Zombie Turkeys is definitely not your typical zombie book. Instead, it is a parody of the standard zombie book, and as such may even be destined for cult status." - Amazon

"I am not one for . . . zombie material, but this was a very entertaining book. The satire kept me reading. Being from Central Illinois I was quite familiar with much of the locations mentioned in the book. I look forward to what is next." – Amazon

"Very fun to read! I enjoyed every part of the book especially a new zombie storyline!" – Amazon

Reviews of *My Undead Mother-in-law,* Volume 2 of Life After Life Chronicles:

"I am a huge zombie fan, I had thought the genre had worked itself out for a while and then I read this book. I think I have been scarred for life! I foresee months if not years of counseling in my future." – Author Greg Aldridge, Goodreads.com

"Who hasn't had mother in law issues? Well, what if your mother in law was a zombie? And yet our hero is a zombie avenging evil with her zombie turkeys, bulls, and corgis--all under her command. Hilarious and heartwarming at the same time. The perfect wedding shower gift for the new bride. . . . Can't wait for Andy's next adventure!"
Jacqueline Gillam Fairchild--author Estate of Mind, The Scrap Book Trilogy – Amazon

"This is the kind of mother-in-law we all need--one who can take over a flock of zombie turkeys by tearing the lead turkey into bite-sized pieces. This is just as good as "Zombie Turkeys," folks! Andy Zack is an amazing author! Hope he writes another story soon!" – Amazon

"My Undead Mother-In-Law, while not publicized as a YA story, should appeal to a generation for whom blogging is part of their daily life. Zach even asked a less than famous blogger to write the humorous "Foreword" to the book. That's really what any reader needs to enjoy this strange yarn—a sense of humor and a willingness to lose yourself in a world that never was and never will be. But a world that seems likely to appear once again in yet another sequel."
- Author Dr. Wesley Britton, BookPleasures.com

The Life After Life Chronicles

by Andy Zach

Zombie Turkeys
My Undead Mother-in-law

MY UNDEAD MOTHER-IN-LAW

Andy Zach

My Undead Mother-in-law: The Family Zombie With Anger Management Issues

Copyright © 2017 by Andy Zach
First Edition, 2017

Cover Illustration and jacket design: Sean Patrick Flanagan
Edited by: Dori Harrell
Formatting by Rik: Wild Seas Formatting
(http://www.WildSeasFormatting.com)
Published by: Jule Inc.

PO Box 10705
Peoria, Illinois 61612
zombieturkeys.com

ISBN: 978-1-9737140-1-9

To my mother-in-law, Barbara Beyer, who lived with us as I wrote this book. You're not a zombie, but you're almost as unusual.

Acknowledgments

First I want to acknowledge my illustrator Sean Flanagan, who did another great job on the book cover. His covers get more comments than my books do!

Next, let me mention my children, Tori, Olivia, Ray, and daughter-in-law Jacki. They help me brainstorm ideas and test my writing and make it better.

Along those lines, I applaud my editor Dori Harrell, who aside from providing professional editing and helpful feedback, also encourages me as an author.

Finally, I always have my wife Julie. She patiently listens to me explode with laughter as I read my own jokes to her and then she suggests how the story could be better.

Foreword

I was completely blown away when Andy Zach asked me to write the foreword to his book. I even protested to him: "Andy! You're a published author! I'm Ron Yardley, a mere amateur blogger."

"It's the least I can do, to give you some publicity when I'm copying many pages of your blog verbatim for my book *My Undead Mother-in-law*."

"But won't people notice the big difference in writing quality between a mere blogger, like me, and an established paranormal author, like you?"

"Nah. I'm not that good. You're probably as good of a writer as I am."

"I've never had any author say such a thing to me!"

"I'm not just any author. But don't get a big head. I haven't told you the main reason I picked you to write my book foreword."

"What's that?"

"You're a blogger. You'll keep it to three hundred words or less."

"Oh."

So that's how I got to write this foreword. I don't think I need to say much about Andy Zach, the foremost paranormal bird and animal author and the only one with a PhD in animal revivification from the prestigious Paranormal Animal College at Cambridge University. You're no doubt aware of his first work, *Zombie Turkeys*, in his Life after Life Chronicles, where he documents the turkey apocalypse that occurred in the US. Andy told me he will continue to write zombie-related books in his Life after Life Chronicles as long as zombies dominate our news cycle.

Let's see: that's two hundred and fifty-seven words. Time to wrap up this foreword.

This is Ron Yardley, writer of "My Undead Mother-In-Law" blog, signing off.

"Never give in, never give in, never, never, never, never—in nothing, great or small, large or petty—never give in"

Winston Churchill

Chapter 1

Gary

"You know I love your mother. But your mother's a zombie. Who wants to see one zombie, let alone four of them?"

"Now that's not fair. Mom and Dad have adjusted to their zombiism very well. Mom still volunteers at church and bakes cookies and pies for the bake sales. Dad still works as an accountant at GM. There's nothing to worry about!"

"That covers Diane and George. I know them. I guess I'm ready for them. What about your brother and this new girlfriend of his? I don't think Don has said two whole sentences to me since I've known him!"

"He'd never get a word in edgewise with you, Ron. You said it yourself—you've had diarrhea of the mouth since you were born. He and his friend Maggie will be fine."

"Whatever you say, Karen." I knew when to surrender. I focused my eyes on the Indiana turnpike ahead.

"Hmmph!"

I glanced at Karen while I drove. Her arms were crossed under her breasts, and she looked out the window, away from me. Trying to make peace, I said, "I thought we dodged a bullet when the zombie turkey plague just missed Gary, Indiana. I never dreamt this zombie thing would hit our own family." I kept my tone neutral

"So far it hasn't hit us hard. Life goes on as usual."

Great! At least she was still talking to me. "As great as it can with glowing red eyes," I said with a big grin.

"I suppose. I hadn't really thought about how hard life would be like that."

"I have no clue what that'd be like."

"Clueless from Toledo!"

"Clueless going to Gary." We laughed. "Remember our rehearsal dinner?" I said.

"Sure. That was six years ago. Hard to believe."

"Your Mom and I got along fine there. We dominated the conversation, as I recall. I hardly noticed the rest of your family. I do remember your dad impressing me with his analytical mind. Did Don even talk? He's like a mute bivalve."

"Yes, a little, to me."

"Well, I don't remember anything. 'I only had eyes for you,'" I warbled.

"Ha! Good thing I didn't hear you sing before I said 'I do.'"

"I'm sure you did."

"I'm sure I wouldn't notice. I was too amazed I got to marry the Big Man on Campus, college graduate, and internet marketer, Ron Yardley."

"So why did a beautiful girl like you marry a guy like me?"

"I still don't think I'm beautiful, just average. You're the good-looking one!"

"Thank you, but you're wrong. You're the good-looking one. I'm just average."

"We'll have to agree to disagree."

We settled into a companionable silence for ten miles or so. Then I said, "I know why I'm so reluctant to meet your family now that they're zombies."

"Why?"

"I did some marketing for the *Midley Beacon* during the turkey apocalypse last Thanksgiving and then later for author Andy Zach's book about it, *Zombie Turkeys*. I saw a lot of bloody photos and videos and read too many gory details. I never liked the idea of pretend zombies, let alone real-life ones. I was just glad we missed it in Toledo. Now I'm in the middle of it."

"Now, Ron, visiting my family, even if they're zombies, doesn't put you in the middle of another zombie apocalypse."

"Yeah, you're right." That was the ultimate solution to any marital disagreement, I'd found. "What's Don's girlfriend's name again?"

"Maggie. Maggie Unsicker. Mom said they were going to announce their engagement this weekend, for Valentine's Day. That's why we're going. Remember?"

2

"Of course. I wonder why so few people have turned zombie? First there were zombie squirrels, then zombie rabbits, then zombie cows, and finally, a dozen people or so turned zombie."

"None of those zombies were really numerous like the turkeys were."

"Thank God for that! What does Maggie do anyway? Besides play video games like Don, I mean."

"Maggie's a phlebotomist and a lab technician at Methodist Hospital in Gary."

"A what?"

"Phlebotomist. She takes blood samples from people and then runs lab tests on them."

As we pulled up in Karen's parents' drive, I was reassured by the sheer normality of their three-bedroom suburban home: green yard partially covered with snow, evergreen bushes, two-car garage. There was no sign zombies lived there. Of course, what sign could I expect? A skull and crossbones and *Beware of Zombies*? Perhaps a biohazard sign?

Diane greeted us at the door. "Hello, my love!" She hugged Karen.

Karen barely flinched as she looked into her mother's bright-red eyes. But she grunted "Ugh!" at the force of her embrace.

"Ease up, Mom."

"Oh, sorry."

"Hello, Mom," I said as I hugged her as hard I as could.

She hugged me back twice as hard.

"Ugh," I grunted too.

Diane still had blond-highlighted brown hair, as she did when I first met her. She'd gained a pound or two though. She smelled of the body talc White Linen. I recognized it because Karen and I bought it for her birthday last year, pre-zombie. And she still wore her cat-eye reading glasses on a chain around her neck.

Diane seated us on the living room sofa. "Supper's on. I have a nice pot roast for us tonight. Donnie and Maggie should be here soon. George!" she called. "The kids are here!"

A heavy tread down the stairs announced George Newby. His eyes shone red too, but while Diane was built like a middle-aged woman, George was a classic wide-body. His shoulders filled the stairway. You'd think he was a truck driver or a lineman rather than an accountant.

"Hi, Karen. Hi, Ron," he rumbled. He hugged his daughter, as if he held a baby bird, and shook my hand without hurting me in his bratwurst fingers. His bright-red eyes looked squarely into mine.

"I'm so glad you made the trip. You can help us put to rest the ugly rumors that people with zombiism aren't human. It's just a disease. It's not even harmful," Diane enthused as she sat across from us. George sat next to her in a brown leather recliner.

"Mom, we love you. You don't have to convince us," I said.

"Of course not. I know that. It's just that we've had people talking behind our backs at church and the public health officials trying to pressure us to get the treatment to eliminate the disease."

"Don't you want to get rid of it? I think the antibiotics for it are safe and effective."

"You'd think so, but we actually have never felt better in our lives! I have more energy than ever, and so does George—right, George?"

"Yup."

"My arthritic aches and pains have completely disappeared, and George's old football knee injury is all better too."

Looking out the window, George said, "Don and Maggie just pulled up."

Entering the room, Don looked like a smaller version of his dad, with the same squat build. Maggie was also short and plump and attractive in a round sort of way.

I'm glad Karen got all the good-looking genes in the family, I thought.

We sat down to dinner. Diane made the delicious pot roast with caramelized onions and mushrooms, mixed with carrots and potatoes. Seeing four pairs of shining red eyes around the table twisted my stomach around the pot roast. I wrestled my stomach into submission and tried not to think about it.

For dessert, we had a New York–style cheesecake decorated with a big heart and *Be My Valentine* on the top. It looked yummy, but that didn't make me feel any better about the zombie apocalypse dinner.

"We have the two old sweethearts, me and George; the recent sweethearts, Karen and Ron; and the new sweethearts, Don and Maggie!" Diane announced enthusiastically. She divided the cake into six equal sections.

"Oh, that's too much for me!" Karen exclaimed.

"OK, how about half?"

"That's fine."

Everyone else ate a big portion of cake. Diane noticed me watching her eat and said, "Our appetite has really picked up recently. We're eating more but not gaining weight."

"That alone gives us reason to stay zombie." Don spoke for the first time. Becoming a powerful zombie really brought Don out of his shell. I didn't expect him to speak at all.

"Yes, we were talking about people pressuring us to get treatment before you came."

"Over my dead body!" Don said fiercely and then laughed at the irony.

"That'd actually be pretty hard to do," Maggie said with a smile.

Zombie jokes arose spontaneously around the Newby's dinner table.

"And now, you two, don't you have an announcement?" Diane gazed at Don and Maggie expectantly.

Maggie looked at Don, raising her eyebrows in question. Or maybe she meant, *She's* your *mother.*

"What did you have in mind, Mom?" Don asked with a frown.

"Didn't you say you'd get engaged this weekend?"

"Yeah, we talked about it, but we don't see the point. We're happy living together."

"You *told* me you'd propose to Maggie this weekend!" Diane's outrage crept into her voice.

"Yeah, but I changed my mind."

"You *promised*!" Diane stood and yelled, "Don't lie to your mother!"

"We're adults." Don stood too. "We're allowed to change our minds. And don't yell at me like a little kid." Don glared at his mother.

"You're adults, but you can't live in adultery. If you ever want to stay in our house, you *have* to get married!"

"We don't *have* to do anything! Let's go, Maggie." Don reached to take Maggie's hand, but Diane rushed to him and grabbed his other hand.

"No, you don't! You won't leave until we settle this and you agree to get married!"

"Don't be silly, Mom. You can't stop me." He tried to push her away, but she clung burrlike to his arm.

"Don't make me angry!" she threatened.

Finally, with a convulsive fling, he pushed her across the room. The wallboard dented where she hit. Don looked startled by his own action.

George suddenly stood up, like a mountain rising from the sea. The chair shot out behind him, hitting the section of the dining room wall near the living room and cracking it.

"Don—" he began, firm as a stone.

"So you want to be rough, do you?" Diane's soft tone was far more chilling than her yelling. Every eye, red and otherwise, focused on her. Diane's eyes narrowed.

George stopped, waiting.

"You asked for it. You're not hurt anyway," Don said. He sounded nervous

"You're not too young to be spanked by your old mom!" Diane yelled and leapt across the room with a single bound and grabbed Don's arm, the one he had pushed her with. With a bone-grinding wrench, she tore it out of its socket. Bright arterial blood jetted across the room. Using the arm as a club, she beat Don in the head with his own arm.

"You!" Thunk! The arm hit his ear.

"Will!" Crack! Don's nose broke.

"Propose!" Splat! The skin split around the bicep of the severed arm.

"You!" Whap! The bloody bicep hit his cheek.

"Will!" Squish! The bicep splashed off his head as it burst under the force of the blow.

"Get!" Ploop! Don's eye popped out as the humerus bone of his arm hit his face.

"Married!" Whack! His cheek split open.

"Before!" Bang! His arm bone sliced his scalp open

"You!" Shatter! Don's teeth broke as his own elbow hit him in the mouth.

"Leave!" Crunch! Don's throat collapsed.

"Here!" Crack! Another blow broke Don's skull.

"Tonight!" Diane held the bloody arm threateningly, but Don lay supine on the floor.

"I'm glad that's settled." Diane sniffed. "Look at this mess! Let's all pitch in and clean it up while Don grows a new arm." Diane tossed the old arm into the kitchen trash. "The mops and rags are in the kitchen, Maggie, Ron, Karen." No one argued.

I began breathing again as I wiped my face clean of splattered blood. It felt good to do something. After dumping Spic-n-Span into the bucket, I mopped the laminate floor. I saw Don's arm socket had already skinned over and a new hand budded from it. As I scrubbed the blood from the floor, I watched from the corner of my eye with morbid fascination as his wrist slowly lengthened to a full-sized arm. My stomach wanted to eject my meal, but my brain felt too numb to react.

Looking up from my red-stained mop, I saw the others had cleared the table and cleaned the spots of blood from the furniture and walls using baby wipes from boxes conveniently placed in the room. George was busy spackling the wall cracks.

Diane again noticed my gaze. "Since we've become zombies, we're always breaking things," she commented. "We aren't fully used to our new strength. I think we should buy stock in the spackling company." She chuckled.

Looking down at her bosom, she said, "Oh my! Look at my reading glasses!" They were cracked and bloody. "That's the second pair I've broken."

"Maggie, I guess we'd better get married," Don said as he stood, rubbing his newly grown arm. All his other injuries had vanished. He didn't sound assertive anymore.

"It seems to be really important to your mom," Maggie said. She made the sentence sound like an "Amen" from a tent revival.

"I'm glad that's settled!" Diane said with a big grin. "When will it be?"

"The justice of the peace is open on Monday," George said.

"We'll be there," Don said. "I'll have to take time off work."

"Me too," Maggie said.

"We'll be there too. Our family needs to be together for these important life events. How about you?" Diane asked us.

"We need to work—" I began.

"But I'm sure we can take the time off!" Karen interrupted me.

I didn't mind.

"Wonderful! How appropriate for Valentine's weekend!"

Somehow, we survived the rest of that evening without further incident. Later I talked with Karen as we got ready for bed downstairs, in Donald's old room.

"So that's a normal zombie family?"

"This never happened before! And I haven't heard about any other human zombies having a fight like that."

"Yeah, but that's my mother-in-law who went berserk. Just being around them scares me."

"She's always had a temper, but she's never been that violent."

"I wonder if the zombiism causes increased violence in people? It certainly does for turkeys and squirrels. Did you read the story about the zombie squirrel killing a hawk?"

"No! What happened?"

"The hawk nabbed the squirrel, as hawks normally do, but in midair, the squirrel revived, ripped open the hawk's belly, bit off its leg, and fell a hundred feet to the ground, where it scampered away unharmed. It was captured on drone video."

"Oh! I begin to understand the countries that restrict US immigration and travel unless they've taken the anti-zombie antibiotic."

"Well, we're on the cutting edge of societal evolution. I don't know where this zombie condition will go, but I can see it making big changes."

"That's why it only exists in the US. No other nation would allow it. Here, people have freedom to be zombies."

"Even so, some are arguing the government should force people to be treated for it."

"What do you think, Ron? Should my parents, and Don and Maggie, be forced to be cured of it?"

"I don't know. I don't know what to think. I'm still kind of shell shocked. Would you mind if I blogged for a while before I go to bed? That always helps me settle down and process the day's events."

"Of course. I know that. Good night!" We kissed.

I kept a daily blog, usually about my job and internet marketing, but also covering personal items. I wrote up the evening's events, but I disguised the zombie family. I just titled the post, "My Dinner with a Zombie Family." I didn't know how people would spin it, as pro- or anti-zombie. I just knew I felt better after I finished. I finally relaxed and went to sleep.

* * *

The next morning Sam Melvin, investigative reporter for the print and e-newspaper the *Midley Beacon*, scanned through his daily internet search on "zombie turkeys," "zombie squirrels," "zombie rabbits," "zombie cows," and "zombie humans." The blog post on a dinner with a zombie family startled him. He knew very few humans turned zombie; of those few, most took the zombie bacteria antibiotic. Almost no news at all surfaced about the few who chose to remain a zombie. He smelled a story.

"Lisa! How would you like a story on zombie humans?" Sam called to Lisa from his office to hers. Since the *Midley Beacon*'s revenue had exploded through its reporting on the zombie turkey plague, they had expanded their downtown (one street) Midley office from one room to four: an office for him and Lisa (hers was bigger), a reception area for visitors, and an open area for *Midley Beacon* reporters.

"Don't yell from your office!" Lisa yelled from her office. "Zombie humans? Of course, cretin! That would be worth millions of hits. You know perfectly well we're barely scraping by at the *Midley Beacon*. We can't live on zombie squirrel stories forever. Zombie humans would be ideal. But there hasn't been any new news on them!" Lisa paused in her reflexive insulting and asked, "What d'ya got?"

"I have a blog post on a dinner with a zombie family."

"Doesn't sound too interesting, unless they're eating people."

"Nope, pot roast. However, a fight broke out between two zombies, a mother and a son."

"Promising! Who won?"

"The mom. She tore off her son's arm and beat him with it."

"Ouch! I assume it grew back?"

"Yes. I think I should visit this blogger and find out about this family."

"Of course you should! Repost the blog story and tell our readers you'll be investigating it today. Where's the blogger live?"

"He lives in Toledo, but he's traveling. He didn't say where. I think he's hiding something, probably the identity of the family."

"Double-plus good! Get on his good side, and get in contact with the family. Offer to pay him for hits on the blog post from the *Midley* site."

"I'm on it!" Sam emailed Ronald Yardley and then did a search for his cell phone number. Quickly finding it, he called him.

"Hello, this is Sam Melvin of the *Midley Beacon*. Is this Ronald Yardley?"

"Yes. Call me Ron. Why are you calling?"

"I read your blog post this morning and found it very newsworthy. We'd like to pay you to post it on our website. We'll pay you for each view it gets."

"I'm surprised it got a reaction so fast! Your offer sounds good, but what's the catch?"

"No catch. We want to build good relationships with key news sources like yourself. There's very little news about people with the zombie disease. Where does this zombie family live?"

"Um, I think I have to protect their privacy."

"OK, but can I at least interview you?"

"Me? I guess so. When would you want to meet?"

"Today."

"Um, we're on vacation right now."

"I will gladly pay you for the interview."

"Let me check with my wife and get back with you."

"That's fine. You can call me at this number, my private cell, or our turkey hotline, 1-800-Z-TURKEY. Or you can email me. Or text me."

"OK. I'll give you an answer today. Bye."

"Lisa!" Sam called again.

"Lout! That's not very professional, calling from one office to another," she complained from her office.

"Sorry," he said as he walked into her office. There was no one else in the room, but after four months of marriage, he'd learned to keep his mouth shut. "I've got Ron's story posted on the *Midley* site, and I'm waiting to hear back from him about the interview today. He is hiding the identity of the zombie family."

"Great! I assume *you'll* be able to interview this family if you promise to protect their privacy. I also assume you'll find out the identity of this family and interview them directly." Lisa looked directly at him.

"Of course." With Lisa, it was always safe to agree.

Sam's phone rang. "Hi, Ron... That's great! Let me write down the address... I'll see you at three p.m.! Bye."

"Where is he?"

"Gary, Indiana. I can be there in three hours."

"One hour if you take the plane."

"I forgot about that! I'll call Dan Cosana now." Sam called the *Midley Beacon's* pilot, and they agreed to meet at the local county airport in half an hour. Sam arranged for a rental car at the Gary International Airport.

Two hours later Sam headed in the rental car toward his meeting with Ron Yardley, at a local coffee shop.

"Hi, you must be Ron." Sam recognized him from the description he gave over the phone and from his pictures on his blog: tall, slim, in his late twenties, in an Abercrombie & Fitch sweatshirt. Sam supposed women would think he was good looking.

"Yes. Are you *the* Sam Melvin? Of the *Midley Beacon*? I've read some of your stories on the zombie turkey crisis. I love how you marketed the *Midley Beacon*! I'm glad to meet you!"

Sam basked in Ron's enthusiastic greeting. He and Lisa had gotten a lot of adulation since the zombie turkey story broke, but Ron seemed sincere, if a little overpowering.

"Thank you, Ron. I'm eager to meet you too. Your blog post had the first details I've seen about zombiism in humans. The nation and the world are starving for details on this condition. All the stories I have read dealt with it occurring and people being treated."

"First of all, I have to have your promise to keep all details private. Hide the city and anything else that might violate these people's privacy."

"Of course. I happened to bring along the contract for our interview. It contains a clause on privacy protection."

"Hmm." Ron read the contract. "A thousand dollars? For the interview?"

"And another thousand for an interview with the zombie family."

"I'll have to check with them."

"Of course. Do you think the privacy clause will protect their anonymity?"

"Looks like it. OK, I'll sign it." After that formality, Ron said, "Go ahead!"

"Let's begin at the beginning. When did you hear about this zombie family?"

"Soon after they turned. My wife and I know them."

"Who else knows they're zombies?"

"I guess their church and workplaces."

"Doesn't it get awkward with the bright-red eyes?"

"They've taken to wearing dark glasses. Everyone just thinks they've suddenly become fashionable."

"Have they experienced much pressure to take the antibiotic?"

"Yes, they have been pushed to take it, from work and church and the local health officials."

"Why haven't they taken it?"

"The older couple is in their late forties, and since they've become zombies, they've never felt better in their lives. The younger couple likes the enhanced strength and weight loss."

"Have they noticed any other differences in being zombies?"

"They eat more. I have noticed they all have a lot more energy, a lot more boldness and aggressiveness, I guess."

"Any personality changes?"

"Everything just seems enhanced. When they get angry, they get really angry. When they're happy, they're really happy."

"Have there been any other violent scenes like the one you blogged about?"

"No. That was a stunner to me."

"OK, that should be enough for now. I have a lot of questions about your relationship to them, what they do for work, how their lives have changed, but those'll wait until I meet them. When can I meet them?"

"I'll talk to them tonight and let you know."

"See you, Ron. Thanks a lot. When I write the story, I won't tell what city we're in. I'll just say, 'a certain Midwest city.'"

"That sounds good. I'll call you tonight."

Later that evening, while Sam was eating a steak dinner at the hotel restaurant, Ron called.

"Hi, Sam."

"Hi, Ron."

"I read your story on the *Midley Beacon*. It was good to see my name in there. Thanks for linking to my blog. My blog hits have more than doubled!"

"Sure thing."

"Good news. The zombie family has agreed to be interviewed tomorrow. They'll have you over for lunch at noon."

"I'll be there!"

Chapter 2

West Peoria

Sam arrived at the zombie family's house promptly at noon the next day. A cheery, smiling, middle-aged women with glowing red eyes greeted him at the door.

"You must be Sam Melvin! I'm so glad to meet you! I read the *Midley Beacon* all through the zombie turkey crisis." She shook his hand vigorously. "I'm Diane Newby."

"You weren't supposed to give your name!" Ron shouted from inside the house.

"Don't worry, Ron, Mrs. Newby. I'll protect your privacy," Sam assured them.

As Diane led Sam to the dining room table, she said to Ron, "Ronnie, I'm thinking of coming out publicly as a zombie advocate. I can't hide it, and I don't want to give it up. We do live in the United States, the home of the free and the brave, don't we?"

Even though Sam had faced thousands of blood-thirsty zombie turkeys, seeing four pairs of shining red eyes seated around the dining room table made his stomach clench. Diane introduced him to George and the newly engaged couple, Don and Maggie.

Ron added, "This is my wife, Karen."

Seeing her green eyes looking up into Ron's brown ones reassured Sam.

"I'm pleased to meet you all!" If he ignored the eyes, Diane just sounded like a normal mom. She made grilled cheese and tomato soup, with salad. He stomach unclenched slightly. Enough for him to eat.

"How has the *Midley Beacon* done since the end of the zombie turkey crisis?" Diane asked him.

"After the zombie turkey plague was brought under control, the *Midley Beacon* has fallen on hard times. We're down to half our reporting staff. Most of our profits come from selling zombie turkey merch online."

"Oh, that makes me want to help you out!" Diane cried.

"Maybe you can. Begin at the beginning. When did your family become zombies?"

"In January, as the zombie animals started appearing. Donnie turned zombie. You were at your video game convention, weren't you?"

"Yeah. I didn't realize what was happening for a while. I just knew I got really excited and full of energy. I thought it was the convention and meeting Maggie."

He smiled at her, the first Sam saw from him. She glowed back, and not just her red eyes.

"When did Maggie become a zombie?"

"During the convention sometime. Do you know, Mags?"

"Hmmm. I was holding your hand even though I had a cut on mine. I like holding your hand." She smiled at Don. "Then by the time we left, the cut was gone."

"I didn't know that! I also had a cut on my hand. Maybe our blood mingled?"

"So we're blood brother and sister?"

"I'd rather be your lov—er, husband," he amended, glancing nervously at his mother.

"When did you realize you had turned into zombies?" Sam prompted. This was getting interesting!

"When we got to the hotel and went into the bathroom, we saw our eyes had turned red. Then the clue phone rang. I put together my excitement, energy, and knocking out the mugger—"

"What mugger?" Sam interrupted.

"We were attacked by a mugger coming out of the convention, heading toward the parking lot. I felt very confident and aggressive and knocked him out with one punch." He paused. "I don't think I've punched anyone since I was a little kid and I punched you, Karen."

"I remember that! You little brat!" Karen said with a smile

"That was because you were tickling me."

15

"This is great information! None of this has been documented before! No one really knows why a few families have turned zombie and no one else," Sam said.

"This is news to us too. None of us have really compared notes before. We just tried to move on with our lives," Diane said.

"I have a theory," George cut in.

"What is it, dear? You've never told me," Diane said.

"I just thought of it. We know the zombie turkeys got the condition from the GMO modified corn from Corn-All. I read it on the *Midley Beacon*'s site." He smiled at Sam. "We'd just had corn bread made from Corn-All."

"That's right—I remember reading the label that night before the convention!" Don said.

"Yes. I read ingredient labels too. What if some of the GMO corn got into that batch? That would explain the very limited infections."

"Lisa and I tracked that GMO corn back to Corn-All and then to the disposal company. All of it was buried in a landfill."

"I'd say some got into their production of corn bread."

"I'll get in touch with my friend at the Turkey Institute and see about getting DNA samples from you. Has anyone taken them before?"

"No. We've kept a low profile since then," Diane said. "Although, I remember volunteering to give blood, and the nurse turned me down. Because of my red eyes. Isn't that discrimination, Mr. Melvin?"

"Call me Sam. I'm no lawyer, but if they thought you were contagious, they would be obligated to prevent contamination of the blood supply." Sam continued with his question. "What changes have you noticed since becoming a zombie?"

"With me, I immediately noticed a much higher level of energy," Diane said.

"Me too!" Don, Maggie, and George chimed in.

"Then, when I was vacuuming, I found I could pick up the couch easily with one hand and vacuum under it. That's been a real time-saver!"

"I had a similar experience," George added. "When my car got a flat tire, I found I could unscrew the lugs with my bare hand, pick up the car without a jack, and change the tire quickly and easily."

"That is amazing!" Sam looked at Maggie and Don. "Anything you've noticed?"

"I can work all day and not get tired. I have more energy than anyone at work. I've gotten compliments from my boss since I've changed." Maggie smiled. "Then I can party all night and go back to work the next day!"

"Can she ever! We go out almost every night to some activity, either gaming, movies, or dining. I never get tired either. We're probably only sleeping two to three hours a night."

"That's pretty much the same for me and George. We also have much greater appetites. Our food bill has doubled, and we like red meat a lot more."

"Don't forget your arthritis is gone and my old football injury no longer hurts," George added.

"I wonder if the zombie bacteria can be used to treat other diseases," Sam wondered aloud.

"I don't see why not! None of us have gotten any colds or flu since we've become zombies."

"And my allergies are gone too," Maggie added.

"As soon as we're done here, I'll contact my research friend and investigate this!"

"Can you put in your article that we zombies just want to get along with everyone?"

"I'll consider it, Diane. Just don't try that with zombie turkeys!"

"I'm sure they'd listen to reason from me. Donnie did," Diane said, looking at Don.

Sam chuckled uncertainly and then stopped. No one else was laughing. Don looked rueful. Maggie looked a little apprehensive.

Ron spoke up. "I'm sure zombie turkeys would only argue with you for a short time, Mom."

Sam remembered Ron's description of the beating Diane inflicted on Don. "Um, do you find you have a higher pain threshold?"

"Why yes. I don't think I've been in pain at all. I've burned myself in the kitchen, but the pain vanished almost immediately."

"Yes. After Mom knocked some sense into me, my arm grew back right away, but I don't really remember much pain."

"Fascinating! I'll get all of this written up tonight and published. I'll contact my research friend and get him to get DNA samples from all of you. And I'll hide your names."

"Don't hide mine, Sam. I'm going to be the zombie advocate and get people to tolerate and respect zombies. You can hide the rest of the family."

"Diane, you should just go by your first name. You don't want them tracking us to our house."

"You're right, George. I'll just go by Diane Sydney, my maiden name, and say that's an alias."

"I won't mention your location," Sam said. "But can I tell my research friend, Dr. Ed Galloway, your real name and address?"

"As long as he is the only one and he agrees to protect our anonymity," George said.

Sam wrote his story in his motel before he went to supper and emailed it to Lisa and their webmaster. He then called Dr. Edwin Galloway of the Turkey Institute, more formally known as the Poultry Research Institute at Northwestern University. They collaborated extensively during the zombie turkey apocalypse.

"Hi, Ed, this is Sam."

"Hi, Sam. What's up?"

"I've got some zombie people who are willing to give DNA samples for research. Can you help get the samples taken?"

"That's wonderful! No research has been done on humans with the zombie condition. Hmmm. I have some contacts who could take the samples. Where do these people live?"

"Gary, Indiana. I'll email you the address and their phone number."

As soon as he hung up, Sam's cell phone rang. Noting it was Lisa, he said, "Hi, sweetheart!"

"No time for that romantic crap. We've got another zombie turkey outbreak!"

"Where?"

"Not far from you. It's a small private turkey farm near Gary, Deviled Turkeys. I've sent you the address."

"Odd name."

"They're bedeviling the family, who's surrounded. They called our turkey hotline. I've already notified the local authorities and the Indiana National Guard. Get the story,

Sam! We're dying for news here. I may have to cut our staff back again."

"You've got a hot story in your in-basket from Gary already, about the zombie family. I've got Dr. Galloway getting DNA samples from them."

"Great! You always pick me up, Sam."

"You're turning into a mushball."

"You have that effect on me. Now, hurry up and get going!" She hung up.

"Bye, Lisa." One tradition hadn't changed since their marriage. She still hung up abruptly, leaving Sam talking into a dead phone.

Sam arrived at the Deviled Turkeys farm in the dark winter evening. Sam could see the National Guard trucks and a couple of police cars along the snowy drive to the barnyard. They had distracted the flock of perhaps a thousand turkeys from attacking the house and were now barely holding their own position.

Sam heard the BANG of shotguns, and the *pop, pop* of rifles and pistols. Why did the police waste their time and ammunition? Those weapons proved ineffective against the zombie turkeys last November.

Grabbing his trusty Flaming Turkey brand flamethrower from the backseat, he approached the line of soldiers.

"Stay away, mister!" an officer yelled over the crackle of gunfire.

Sam noticed he had a skinny neck and a shock of red hair.

"You should have a flamethrower!" Sam yelled back.

"We do! We can't use them this close to the buildings. There's a family in there!"

Good thing Lisa isn't here, Sam thought. During the zombie turkey apocalypse, she'd flamed first and asked questions later.

Another car pulled up in the drive. The officer yelled, "Get away, ma'am! This is a dangerous situation!"

"I've come to reason with the turkeys," Diane Newby yelled back, her red eyes gleaming.

"You can't reason with crazed killer turkeys!"

"You watch me!" She leapt past the officer, past the line of soldiers, directly toward the mass of turkeys. The soldiers ceased firing, for fear of hitting her. The mass of turkeys washed over Diane like a tsunami. Sam reluctantly filmed her last moments, for her family's sake.

The mound of turkeys burst apart, revealing Diane throttling a tom. She ripped off its head, legs, wings and then smashed the body into paste on the ground.

"Listen up, you turkeys!" she yelled. "I'm the boss turkey now! Follow me!" Obediently, the turkeys followed her into the barn. She led them back into their cages and shut them in. Where the turkeys had burst doors and wire fencing, using her bare hands Diane wove the tough steel wire into a tight net, holding them securely. "Good thing I'm handy with macramé," she said to herself as she wove.

Diane's clothing was shredded and bloody like she'd been through a wood chipper, but her skin showed pink and unbroken through the many holes in her pants and coat. Sam ran to her.

"Are you OK, Diane?"

"Never felt better! I told you I could reason with the zombie turkeys!"

"How did you find out?"

"It was on the zombie turkey Twitter feed on the *Midley Beacon* page, where I was reading your story about us!"

"Ma'am, I have to thank you for saving us from a difficult situation," the officer said. "I'm Sergeant Coxcomb."

"How appropriate," Sam murmured. Louder, he said, "I'm Sam Melvin, investigative reporter for the *Midley Beacon*."

Smiling broadly, Diane said, "I'm Diane New—er—Sydney. I came here as soon as I heard of the attack. I just knew I could control the zombie turkeys. They're quite easy, compared to children!" She laughed.

"Diane, I filmed your battle. Do I have your permission to broadcast it?"

"By all means! Be sure to say a zombie human came to the rescue! Just call me anytime you have a zombie animal outbreak!"

"Will do!"

"I'll testify to that!" Sergeant Coxcomb said.

"OK, let me interview you then, Sergeant, and I'll add your testimony."

The interviews with Sergeant Coxcomb and Diane, combined with the thrilling video of human zombie versus turkey zombies, burst across the internet like a nuclear bomb. Once again, the *Midley Beacon* plowed new ground in the zombie news business.

The Midley Beacon bought Diane Sydney a new winter wardrobe with its new profits from her story.

A week later, another zombie animal outbreak occurred.

Richard Felix, the owner of Prairie Cattle Farm of West Peoria, surveyed the fifty head of cattle grazing on the hills of his farm in the Kickapoo River Valley on a frosty February morning. A flicker of motion caught his eye to the left.

One of his cows bawled as a long brown body leapt upon the cow's back, ran toward the head, and savagely ripped off her ear. Dozens more of the animals attacked the cow's udder and underbelly.

Dumbfounded, Richard stared as the bleeding cow crumpled to her knees. Were those giant weasels? Rats? He couldn't quite place them, although they seemed familiar. He ran to the barn and grabbed his shotgun. By the time he came back, the cow had been reduced to a bloody skeleton. Its furry attackers were nowhere to be seen.

Shaking, he dialed the Zombie Turkey Hotline with difficulty. He didn't know who else to call.

"Zombie Turkey Hotline, Sam Melvin here."

"Help! Something attacked one of my cows and ate it alive!"

"What? Calm down. Tell me the whole story."

"There's not much more to tell. I was looking at my cows this morning in the field, and I saw one get attacked by dozens of furry brown somethings."

"I'll be right there." West Peoria was just a half an hour from Midley.

Sam found Richard in the middle of his field, studying the cow skeleton with another man.

"Hi, I'm Sam Melvin, investigative reporter for the *Midley Beacon.*"

"Thanks for coming. I'm Richard Felix, the owner of Prairie Cattle Farm. This is Steve Cole, our local animal control officer."

"Hi. What have you found out?"

"Whatever it was, was amazingly savage. It was like a pack of land piranhas," Steve said.

"Did you get any footprints?"

"No. Between the churned mud and the frozen ground, I couldn't find anything identifiable. They were brown furry quadrupeds with sharp teeth, weighing thirty to forty pounds," Steve said.

"How are you going to catch them?"

"I assume they're some kind of zombies. No natural animal acts like that. I'll stake out another cow tonight, surround her with a ring of gasoline, and burn the crap out of them," Richard said.

"Say, I've got an idea," Sam said.

"What's that?"

"Mind if I bring a friend who might be able to control these animals?"

"Good luck with that! They're killers! You see this skeleton? That cow weighed a thousand pounds, and it was reduced to that in two minutes. I wouldn't want that to happen to your friend."

"Somehow, I don't think that'll happen to her. You see, she's a zombie, Diane Sydney. She controlled a flock of zombie turkeys last week."

"Yeah, I think I read something about that. I want her to sign a liability release form if she wants to try anything. I can't guarantee anyone's safety on my farm now. You too, Sam, if you stay overnight."

"OK. Will do." By this time, dangerous zombie situations no longer fazed Sam.

Sam flew Diane in from Gary on the *Midley Beacon*'s plane. She arrived at the Peoria International Airport, private aviation, where their plane was based. Sam met her on the cold, dark tarmac. She smiled to the point of wrinkling her red eyes, showing excitement.

"Hi, Sam! Thanks for flying me in. I've never been in one of these single-engine planes before! I'm thrilled you called me! I'm sure I can deal with whatever these zombies are. I'd hate to see another cow lose its life."

"You know these things stripped a cow to its bones in two minutes?"

"No problem! It'll take me less than two minutes to assert my dominance."

"Good luck—you'll need it."

"No luck—just good old zombie perseverance!"

Sam adjusted his night-vision goggles, and he, Diane, and Richard took turns watching the poor old bovine staked out in the field, near where the other cow had died, from an outbuilding. As the gray morning dawned, the furry creatures attacked the cow.

"Oh no you don't!" Diane shouted and sprang into action. She covered the fifty yards to the cow in world-record time, especially over frozen, snowy ground. She grabbed two of the creatures and smashed their heads together with a splat, like two tomatoes bursting. Dozens of them jumped upon her.

"Which!" Diane grabbed two more from her back, hanging on with their teeth, and hurled them so hard into the frozen ground they each made a red-lined crater.

"One!" She batted two attacking from the front into an oak tree thirty feet away, where they fell, broken.

"Is!" With her other leg, she kicked one biting her calf. It landed a hundred yards away, breaking the ice on the frozen Kickapoo Creek.

"The!" Diane clapped her hands together on one leaping for her throat. The body collapsed with a spray of blood, coating her from head to toe and spraying twenty feet away.

"Boss!" The remaining creatures cowered before her savagery. There was at least three dozen remaining. They rolled over on their backs, exposing their bellies in submission.

"Oh, aren't you cute!" Diane exclaimed, wiping blood and gore from her face, cleaning her hands in the snow and petting the nearest animal.

Carefully, Sam and Richard approached Diane and the unknown beasts. Richard was wide eyed, perhaps more afraid of Diane than of the creatures. Sam had seen Diane in action before, but she still awed him.

"Why, they're corgis!" Sam exclaimed. "They *are* cute—when they're not eating cows. Even with red eyes."

Sam called Lisa later that morning, and when he told her the identity of the pack of animals, she said, "Ah! I thought there was a connection."

"What?"

"That previous day, I read a news story from Hanna City. The Queen Elizabeth Kennels lost fifty of their corgis when they escaped from their fenced-in area. Go there next, Sam, and find out if they had any Corn-All grain in their dog food."

"I'll go there now, with Diane."

The Queen Elizabeth Kennels specialized in breeding Pembroke Welsh corgis. They had been devastated by the loss of their entire breeding stock and had hired trackers to find them, to no avail. When Richard, Sam, and Diane drove up in the Prairie Cattle Farm truck and led the fifty zombie corgis into their kennels, kennel owner Heather Mallorn was astonished.

"They became zombies! No wonder they tore through the fence!" Heather exclaimed.

"No worries now," Diane said with a smile. "I'm the top dog!"

Heather gawked at the red-eyed middle-aged woman.

"You see, this is Diane Sydney. She's a zombie who specializes in taming zombie animals," Sam explained

"How do you do it?" Heather wondered.

"I just assert myself over the pack leader. In this case, I threw him into an oak tree."

"How can I thank you?"

"Please promote my Society of People Equality with Zombies, or SPEwZ, movement. I want zombie people to be treated with the same respect as every other person in this great country. Here's my card with my website."

"I'll do that. I respect you!"

"Thank you. That means so much to me."

Sam recorded Heather telling of the loss of her corgis and Diane rescuing them. He noticed the eight dogs that Diane smashed had completely regenerated and were following her.

Sam asked Heather, "Could I see the dog food you used, especially any recently purchased or opened?"

"Sure." There were the usual bags of Chicken Soup for the Dogs, IAMS, and other common brands, but nothing from Corn-All.

"Do you ever feed them table scraps?"

"Never! But the other day, they got into a bag of corn meal I just bought. In fact"—she paused—"that was the day before they escaped."

"Could I see that bag?"

"Here it is."

Corn-All Corn Meal, read the label.

"That's what I was looking for! Could I take this bag for analysis? I think this caused your dogs to go zombie."

"By all means! I will never buy another thing from Corn-All if that's the case!"

Sam took the bag, packed it into a box, and shipped it to Dr. Edwin Galloway of the Turkey Institute. He wrote up the story and uploaded his videos and then called Lisa.

"Hi, Sam!" Lisa answered. "Another great job! We're in the money! Our website hits have spiked, as has our paper's subscriptions. We've got the national media eating out of our hands! Plus, our zombie merch and turkey trap sales are higher than ever!"

"Good news! Do you think we can add a blog for Diane to advocate for SPEwZ, Society of People Equality with Zombies?"

"Better than that, I'll send our newly hired videographer over to her weekly to record a vlog, which we'll host on our website."

"Wonderful! I'm sure she'll be delighted."

The SPEwZ vlog proved so popular that HBO and Netflix competed to host Diane's own reality show, *Life-Saving Zombies*. Netflix finally won, and SPEwZ became the latest cause célèbre. Ellen and Oprah each hosted Diane Sydney.

Dr. Galloway's friend at the Mayo Clinic, Dr. Marchanne Herbst, tested the Newbys' DNA and confirmed all of the standard zombie abilities: quick regeneration through the human zombie bacteria, E. coli Homo Zapiens (ECHZ). The regenerated tissue was twice as strong as previously. Existing chronic conditions, such as arthritis, degenerating cartilage, inflammation, all disappeared as the mutable bacteria replaced the damaged tissue.

Dr. Marchanne also discovered why zombie eyes glowed red: they had a layer of blood vessels that reflected the light and enabled zombies to see in the dark. The tissue was exactly like animals' reflective tapetum lucidum behind their retinas that helps them see in the dark. Dr. Herbst wrote a paper on human zombies, classifying them as a subspecies of human, Homo Zapiens. In it she noted differences between zombie turkeys and humans. ECHZ could not be spread pneumatically, but only through blood contact. It was much more resistant to salt water and antibiotics but could be cured through massive doses.

This medical finding sparked a frenzied medical race to develop zombie-based treatments. However, Diane Sydney didn't wait for the ponderous medical community to develop FDA-approved medicines. She short cut the whole industry by selling one-milliliter ampoules of zombie blood to be injected. She copied the EpiPen design and substituted zombie blood for antihistamine, thus bypassing the patent. (Their patent attorneys never thought of patenting zombie blood injections.) This came with the guarantee to turn the recipient into a zombie, with no promise of curing anything. She donated the blood from her, her husband, and son and daughter-in-law under strict medical supervision. And the cures poured in.

Two liters of blood donated by the four zombies made two thousand ampoules. They kept their guarantee; everyone became a zombie.

The FDA and medical community were outraged. But there was little they could do. Under Maggie's professional supervision, they collected the zombie blood safely. The blood turned people zombie, as guaranteed. And zombiism cured diseases. Alzheimer's was reversed. Elderly on their deathbeds rose up and walked out of the sanitariums. Further, amputees regrew limbs. Cerebral palsy patients tossed their walkers and canes and danced away. Muscular dystrophy and ALS, myasthenia gravis, and leukemia and cancer of all kinds fell before the zombie blood.

The demand for zombie blood grew. Athletes turned themselves zombies to improve their performance. A zombie broke the three-minute mile. Another lifted a thousand pounds over its head. Quickly, the NBA, NFL, MLB, and NHL banned zombies from competing, as did the international soccer league FIFA and the IOC.

With her own family tapped out on giving blood, through SPEwZ Diane formed a network of zombies who donated blood for others. The demand far exceeded the supply even then, but Diane kept the price down to a hundred dollars per ampoule. She split the profit with whoever donated. This provided a good living to zombies just giving blood. The zombies also discovered, unlike regular humans, zombie humans could donate a liter of blood per day, with no ill effects. Still, even with hundreds of liters of zombie blood arriving daily, they could not keep up with the millions of requests.

Diane prioritized the blood requests into life threatening and non-life threatening. George quit his job with GM to incorporate and run their booming business. Even then, they were barely able to keep up with life-threatening requests.

The zombie debate reached the halls of Congress. Some proposed bills to make zombies illegal, and others proposed zombie-rights bills. Nothing got passed in the acrimonious debate. The pro- and anti-zombie division split the political parties. Those with diseases and disabilities wanted the zombie blood. They hailed it as a universal cure-all and clamored for the government to support zombies and give them full rights.

The more fearful and the established medical community warned of unknown side effects of zombiism. The FDA and the pharmaceutical companies were shaken to their foundations by this simple, inexpensive cure. Medical insurance companies also joined with them, seeking to ban zombie blood altogether. The proponents of government health care generally opposed the zombie cure since it sucked out the need for government intervention. They lobbied heavily in the senate and house to make zombie blood illegal. Lawyers across the country profited from representing both sides in lawsuits and countersuits.

The congressmen were stunned into indecision, torn between millions of campaign dollars waved in front of them and millions of voters clamoring for more zombie blood cures. The Republican and Democratic parties themselves split down the middle over the zombie issue. The whole country was in a turmoil but paralyzed politically.

The *Midley Beacon* had never been more popular or more prosperous. They were the known authority on all things zombie. Lisa rehired all their laid-off reporters and doubled their staff and then doubled it again, to over a hundred employees. Their website had more traffic than CNN, *WSJ*, ABC, NBC, and CBS combined. Their YouTube videos alone surged past a billion hits worldwide.

* * *

Vik Staskas absently stroked his long glossy-black hair as he skimmed through the day's news on his wall-mounted monitor from his five-hundred-foot superyacht. He noted the surge in zombie cures and sought to tap into the money. He hired operatives to infiltrate the *Midley Beacon* and SPEwZ Inc., the business arm of the famous charitable zombie organization. The possibility of failure didn't occur to him. He succeeded in everything he tried: a street thief as an orphan in Belgrade; a college student in Paris, where he got his PhD in robotics; and taking over European organized crime without the nominal bosses knowing he existed. He was ready to take over the US.

He developed remote-controlled cyborg animals and insects. He used them to spy, to infiltrate, to conquer, to steal, to kill. They were unstoppable. He planned his first hijacking of a zombie blood air shipment from Gary, Indiana. He could think of several practical uses for cyborg-controlled zombies in his crime empire. As they were, zombies had too much free will for his taste. He chuckled. Even zombies didn't stand a chance against him.

Chapter 3

Los Angeles

My Undead Mother-In-Law Blog—November 15, 2016, by Ron Yardley

"Hello, world!" I wrote into my blog. I sat in my home office in my Herman Miller chair as I did each evening before bed. "My life is great today! The now booming economy, stimulated by the optimism and the new zombie blood cure, has put the whole country in a good mood. Even Republican and Democrat lawmakers are cooperating.

"The zombie woman I've been writing about, Diane Sydney, finally got her zombie equality bill passed by Congress! I think enough people have become zombies and enough people are sympathetic to their cause that the political parties have caved in to the voters before the November election.

"Diane's zombie blood business, SPEwZ Inc., together with her nonprofit organization, SPEwZ, has cornered the market on zombie blood cures. Despite increasing their supply through millions of new zombies donating blood, demand has passed ten million doses per month. That's just for people with fatal diseases or injuries. Since Diane Sydney is a close friend, I'm thrilled for her. But I'm also delighted at the millions of lives being saved. It's like an inverse zombie apocalypse: millions of lives are being saved, not killed! This makes up for the deaths caused by the zombie turkey attacks, which began a year ago.

"In fact, you could call this a new golden age of zombies.

"Diane Sydney has purchased the pack of zombie corgis and uses them to quell any zombie outbreak. Zombie agents occupy each airline flight and prevent any hijacking. No one wants to tackle a zombie. The whole genre of zombie fiction has changed from rotting undead to zombies as superheroes."

I looked at what I'd written. It was OK, not great. Two hundred and fifty words. It should be longer, for maximum SEO impact. But I was too tired, and I wanted to get to bed before Karen fell asleep.

* * *

Ben Sawyer, an independent truck driver, closed his truck's rear door on a load of zombie blood ampoules, sealed it, and left SPEwZ Inc. for the Gary International Airport. As an independent hauler who'd gotten this run with the lowest bid, it had become his favorite milk run. Although Gary traffic could be hairy, the distance was short, and he usually finished in less than an hour. He just had to be careful the truckload was sealed and untampered when he transferred it to the air carrier.

The seal was fine when he dropped it off at the cargo building. He watched workers transfer the sealed containers into the plane while he had a coffee. The truckloads of the shipments from SPEwZ Inc. had ballooned from weekly to daily over the six months he'd had this run. The zombie blood went all over the US, and he knew many people slipped into the US for the zombie treatments as well.

Something scuttled into the cargo hold of the plane. It looked like a rat. Yuck. Not his problem though. Then a snake slithered in. The stevedores loading the plane with lift trucks hadn't been looking. He'd better tell someone.

He walked to the door to the tarmac where he had dropped his trailer. "Hey, buddy!"

"What?" one of the men replied.

"I saw a rat and a snake go onto that plane."

"Huh. We'll look into it."

His duty done, Ben finished his coffee and went on to his next job.

The men looked carefully through the cargo compartment but didn't find anything. Nor did their boss. He mentioned it to the pilot, Jed Yager, who looked concerned. Jed carefully examined the whole plane. Nothing. The animals probably slipped off again. Or maybe the snake ate the rat and was sleeping it off. Or it could have been someone's wild imagination. Rats and snakes on a plane just weren't natural.

Jed had a flight plan to follow. He took off at noon, headed for Dallas–Fort Worth. That was the main distribution point for the zombie blood for the entire southern US. Halfway there, his copilot, Sarah Lagrange, yelled, "Yow! What bit me?" She reached with her left hand for her right shoulder blade.

Glancing over, Jed was just in time to see a large olive-gray snake drop to the floor of the cockpit. "A snake!" he yelled. Fortunately, he'd set the plane to autopilot.

Jed was one of the few pilots trained and authorized to use the .40 federally issued handgun in the cockpit. He drew it and looked for the snake.

Sarah moaned, "Oh, I feel terrible."

"Crap." He had to help Sarah first. He pulled out his knife, cut Xs in both puncture wounds, and sucked out the blood and venom. Sarah passed out. No sign of the snake.

While he was looking for the snake, Sarah wheezed, sighed, and died.

He returned the pilot's chair and was about to radio air traffic control about Sarah's death, when he heard a strange voice behind him say, "Don't radio." It was a little tinny voice, like through an old-fashioned radio. He whirled around to see a large rat staring at him. To add to its strangeness, the rat wore a metal yarmulke.

"Who—what are you?"

"I'm your best friend. Only I can keep the snake from biting you too."

"Where's the snake?"

"At your feet, one-tenth of a second away from striking you. You must obey me exactly in order to stay alive."

Glancing down, Jed saw the same olive-gray snake that had killed Sarah at his feet, its fangs bared. It hissed.

"What do you want?"

"Land immediately at the Manhattan airport in Kansas."

Shaking with fear, Jed scanned the approach vectors. He didn't have much time to reroute. He was already over Saint Louis. He banked to the west. "We'll be there in less than an hour." He felt silly talking to a rat, but he mostly did it to calm himself down.

"I know."

"I'll have to radio air traffic control to let them know of the change in route."

"Don't, if you wish to live."

"O...K." Quietly, subtly, he set the aircraft's transponder to 7500, the hijacking signal. Nothing happened.

"The transponder's been hacked, so it only transmits normal signals."

Frantically, he keyed the radio mike. "Mayday! Mayday!" The radio was dead.

"I disconnected your radio before the mamba struck. Now, do you wish to live or die?"

He supposed he could crash the plane and kill them all, but he didn't have it in him. "Live."

"Land at the Manhattan airport, and I won't kill you."

The rest of the journey passed in silence. After they landed, the rat said, "Pull up to the military ramp."

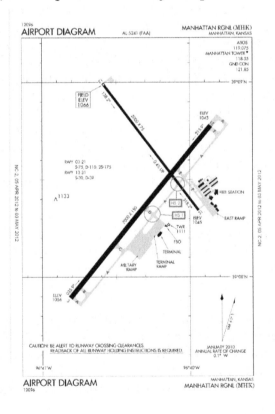

"Landing without announcing will cause the police and military to come."

"I know. That's why this plane was announced to air traffic controller in Manhattan as a top-secret military cargo plane."

"How? How can you do all this?"

The rat remained silent.

Jed parked the plane at the military ramp. He felt the cargo doors open and the plane being unloaded.

"I will leave you now. You may depart." Quickly, the rat scuttled out the cockpit door

With a ragged sigh, Jed walked out the door. A sharp burning pain struck his calf.

"That dirty rat—" Blackness took him.

Silent men in military fatigues carried the two bodies away. The cyborg animals rode in the back of the National Guard truck, providing security for the cargo. None of the hired help would dare to steal from the Boss, but the Boss wanted to be sure that no one would hijack his zombie blood.

* * *

The *Midley Beacon* office hummed with activity. Lisa purchased a whole building on Main Street in Midley. There were offices for Sam (now senior investigative reporter), Lisa (now editor and founder with a corner office), and a large work area with workstations for twenty-four reporters. Most of the reporters were out covering various aspects of animal and human zombiism in the US and worldwide. However, a half dozen typed busily at their laptops and chatted at the coffee machine. Sam directed their efforts and collated their reports, with plenty of input from Lisa. The whole basement was devoted to printing. The second floor held storage and computer servers and their IT staff. Meanwhile, in the lot behind the building, a new facility was rising.

They heard the noise of construction even though the office was tightly shut like an air-conditioned fortress against the blazing heat of a typical Illinois August.

"Lisa!" Sam shouted from his office.

"Moron! How many times must I tell you to act professionally now that we're a big business?" Sighing with exasperation, Lisa said as he entered, "Would it really kill you to walk into my office first, without yelling?"

"Sorry, Lisa," Sam said with a hang-dog expression. "It's just I'm so excited about a breaking story from Kansas!"

"What?"

"An airplane of zombie blood was hijacked yesterday, and the entire cargo was stolen."

"Unbelievable! How did it happen?"

"No one quite knows. The airplane deviated from its flight plan, was announced as a secret military plane to the Manhattan air traffic controllers, landed, and was unloaded into a National Guard truck."

"What does the crew say?"

"No crew was found on the plane. The military knew nothing about this, nor the truck. There were no plates or identification on the truck. All that's left is an empty 737 and two missing pilots."

"A mystery! Should Lashon Miller investigate this?"

Lashon was an ace reporter from their zombie turkey story. She had married turkey-caller entrepreneur Rulon Miller after last Thanksgiving's zombie turkey outbreak and now lived in south Chicago.

"She's off reporting on discrimination against zombies and the Congressional efforts to make them a protected group. There's over a million in the US now. I think she's in Washington DC."

"How about Charlie Gomez?" Charlie Gomez was one of their first reporters hired for the zombie turkey plague. He had bravely reported on the Battle of Soldier Field in Chicago.

"He's down in Texas reporting on the use of zombie blood to help people lose weight. That program will be affected by this hijacking, for most of the blood of this shipment was for that purpose."

"Hmmm. Call Charlie and tell him to add in the hijacking angle—how will it affect people? The research program? How will they get replacement blood? Is it covered by insurance?" Lisa smiled. "For the mystery, let's you and I go together! It'll be like a third honeymoon!"

"Lisa, every day with you is like a honeymoon."

"When you say it like that, I believe you. Make the arrangements, and we'll leave today. Let me know if we're leaving from Peoria or Bloomington. Pick whichever one gets us to Manhattan faster."

"Will do."

Unnoticed in the drop ceiling above, a small chipmunk listened carefully. It wore a metal yarmulke like the rat on the airplane.

Hundreds of miles away, Vik Staskas smiled to himself. Nothing like bringing his objects of interest directly into his reach. Vik was not a sentimental man, but he had a fondness for his cyborg chipmunks since they were the first cyborg animals he had created for his PhD. A computer chip listened, saw, and transmitted via 4G cell phone network to his cell or the nearest computer screen in his network.

While one chipmunk listened above Lisa's office, another had chewed a hole in the ceiling and watched Lisa's office and her large computer screen. Vik whimsically named them Alvin and Theodore.

Vik also tapped the *Midley Beacon*'s wireless network, tracking all their communication. He filtered the mass of data into Input, In Process, Output, and Intraoffice Communication. To cover any holes in his surveillance, he planted one of his people in the *Midley Beacon* IT group to send him the passwords to all the computers and network. His goal was to know what they knew when they knew it or sooner, to anticipate their actions, and influence them to his benefit. Knowing Sam and Lisa's plans allowed him to prepare for them and lead them appropriately.

* * *

That evening, Sam and Lisa left for Manhattan, Kansas, by a leased jet directly from Peoria. Arriving in Manhattan two hours later, the airport manager, Art Bochel, greeted them.

"Hi, Mr. Bochel. We're from the *Midley Beacon*. I'm Lisa Melvin, and this is my husband, Sam."

"Hi, Lisa and Sam. Call me Art. I feel like I know you already. I love the *Midley Beacon*! How can I help you?" Art spoke with breathless enthusiasm.

"What can you tell us about the plane hijacking?"

"Not much at all. Our air traffic controller got a special message on a military channel about a top secret cargo plane coming in. We allowed the plane to land and a National Guard truck to pick up its cargo. We've looked at the security video. No faces were recognizable. The uniforms were Kansas

National Guard, but there were no identifiable markings. And the National Guard truck also was unmarked."

"Yowza," Sam said. "That's not a lot to go on."

"Can we look at the videos?" Lisa asked.

"Sure."

They sat at a screen in the security room and replayed the grainy videos several times. They could tell nothing about the men. Then they looked at the images of the truck. There seemed to be nothing, but Lisa said, "Hey, play it again, Sam."

Sam obliged.

"Look at where the license plate should be."

"It's blacked out. So what?"

"That means they covered it up. What if it really is a National Guard vehicle that they stole and then returned?"

"Seems farfetched."

"Let's go to the nearest National Guard base and see if we find one."

"We've come this far—we might as well."

"Say, before you go, can I get your autographs?" Art asked.

"Sure," Sam said.

"And a selfie?"

"Why not?" Sam and Lisa obliged their fan.

The nearest National Guard camp was in Manhattan, but it was closed. "Let's look around anyway," Lisa said.

Walking around the outside perimeter fence, they saw some trucks parked. "I'd like to look at their license plates, to see if there's any black tape left on any of them," Lisa said

"How will we get in?"

"We could wait until the morning, or we could climb over the fence."

Sam eyed the razor wire above the ten-foot fence. "Not going to happen."

"Let's see how close we can get to the trucks and look at them through the night-vision goggles."

They walked a half mile around the camp to the fence just behind the trucks. Sam used his goggles.

"I can't quite see if those marks are tape or scratches or what." He pressed up against the fence, then shouted, "Holy cow!"

"What's up, Sam?"

"Look!" He pressed against the fence and it lifted up. The fence had been neatly cut along the outside of the poles and was only attached at the top. The cuts were completely invisible from the inside and barely visible from the outside. The cut section was big enough to drive a truck through.

"I'd say you found a way in, Sam—*the* way in the hijackers probably used." They slipped in and closely examined the plates of the trucks. One had scraps of black tape on it.

"Let's turn this truck inside out."

Inside the back of the truck, they found some scraps of packing and shrink wrap. In the cab they found nothing.

"Hmmm. If anything, this cab is too neat, like it's just been cleaned," Lisa said. She dug into the cushion next to the driver's seat. "What's this? Pay dirt!"

"What is it?"

"A thumb drive! Let's get back to our car and see what's on it."

"No logo on the drive?"

"Nope. Just plain black."

In their car, Lisa plugged it into her laptop and opened it up. "Two files: plan A and plan B." Opening the first, she read. "Four p.m. plane leaves. Five p.m. Saint Louis take over. Six p.m. arrive in Manhattan. Transfer cargo. Clean up the plane. Six thirty p.m. depart for the base. Seven p.m. arrive at the base. Twelve a.m. return truck."

"No addresses? Names?"

"Nope. But we know their base is within a half hour of Manhattan by truck."

"What's plan B?"

"Let's see. Six thirty p.m. *Stella Moru* departs Port of LA. Seven thirty p.m. take over the ship, divert to rendezvous. Nine thirty p.m. Transfer cargo. Ten thirty p.m. clean up the ship."

"What's the *Stella Moru*?"

"Let's see." Searching the internet, Lisa read, "Container ship, registered in Liberia. Goes from Los Angeles to China and back."

"So it's a real ship, leaving at six thirty p.m. Pacific time. What date?"

"Schedule. November twenty-third, leaving for China. That's tonight!"

"That's now! Can we call them and warn them?"

"You call, and I'll drive us to the airport. We'll fly right to LA."

Sam called as Lisa drove at high speed back to the airport, somehow managing to avoid the police.

"Los Angeles port authority, this is Jerry Filbert, associate manager."

"Hello, there is a danger of a ship hijacking of the *Stella Moru*."

"How do you know? Who is this anyway?"

"This is Sam Melvin, investigative reporter for the *Midley Beacon*. We were investigating a plane hijacking here in Manhattan, Kansas, and we found evidence from the hijackers that they planned to take over the *Stella Moru*."

"Sam Melvin? *Midley Beacon*? I think I can believe you if you are indeed the famous Sam Melvin. What is this hijacking plan?"

"Reading it as we found it: 'Six thirty p.m. *Stella Moru* departs Port of LA. Seven thirty p.m. take over the ship, divert to rendezvous. Nine thirty p.m. transfer cargo. Ten thirty p.m. clean up the ship.'

"It's six forty-five Pacific time, so the ship should be on the way out now."

"Hmmm. Yes, they just departed. I'll radio them now."

"Mind if I stay on the phone and find out what happens?"

"OK."

Lisa and Sam arrived at the airport. Sam walked to the plane with his cell phone glued to his ear. Dan Cosana filed the flight plan and took off.

"We can't contact the *Stella Moru*!" Jerry Filbert said with a frantic note in his voice.

"Can you send the coast guard after them?"

"Let me try."

Fifteen minutes later, Sam heard, "OK, the coast guard is going after them. They should reach them in about forty-five minutes."

"Hmmm. That's eight p.m. The schedule says they will be taken over and diverted in fifteen minutes! Can you send a plane to look for them?"

"I'll try."

After another fifteen minutes, Jerry came back and said, "OK, the coast guard agreed to search for them. The plane should be over them in twenty minutes.

"I hope they reach them in time!"

"It's pretty hard to hide a whole ship."

* * *

The container ship *Stella Moru* departed slowly from the Port of Los Angeles, heading to China with a load of cell phones, computers, and IT equipment worth hundreds of millions of dollars. The captain, Dimitri Koumondoros, looked out over his ship from the stern tower after completing his launch checklist. The *Stella*, as the crew called her, was a Panamax-class ship with a capacity of 4,200 shipping containers. He had 3,954 on board for his trip to Shanghai.

About an hour out from Los Angeles, Dimitri sat in his cabin, studying the weather ahead, when he heard a knock.

"Come in!" English was the ship's language. The thirty-member crew hailed from many countries, and most everyone knew some English.

The knob slowly turned, and to his astonishment, a capuchin monkey entered, wearing what seemed to be a metal yarmulke. After jumping on his desk, the monkey handed him a map.

"Hello. I'm taking over this ship. Please steer the ship to this point in the ocean. Don't tell the crew."

The tinny voice came from the metal yarmulke. It sounded like a cell phone in speaker mode. Too startled to talk, the captain took the map. The coordinates pointed to an area about fifty miles off their course, south of Santa Rosa Island.

"Why should I listen to a monkey?" He felt silly talking to the monkey, but he assumed it had some kind of radio in its metal cap.

"Because there is a black mamba at your feet."

Dimitri quickly looked under his desk. A large olive-gray snake coiled there, fangs bared, ready to strike. Sucking in a gasp of air, Dimitri slowly edged his chair backward.

"Do not move any further, or you will die. Issue the order to change course, and you will live."

He eyed the radio and the intercom on his desk. "I'll have to call the pilot."

"Call him in here, but say nothing more than, 'Come to my cabin. I have a course change.' Then give him the map. Any other word is death. Any attempt to send a distress signal is death. If you fail me, I'll kill you and try your first mate."

Dimitri swallowed and called the pilot and gave him the new course. When he was gone, he said, "I'm going to have to go to the head."

"The snake will follow you, to ensure you do not signal anyone."

"How do you control the snake?"

The monkey gave no answer, but Dimitri saw a metal yarmulke on top of the snake's head, as it followed him. He could barely pee, with a poisonous snake curled at his feet.

Nervously, he said to the snake, "You don't talk, do you?"

"Shut up and pee," the snake said in a gravelly voice.

The voice came from the metal yarmulke.

Once back at his desk, Dimitri asked the monkey, "Will I stay here the whole voyage? The crew will become suspicious."

"When we reach our destination in two hours, you may leave."

"That's in the middle of nowhere, off the standard shipping paths!"

No answer. However, the monkey pulled out a sandwich from its backpack and ate it, watching him the whole time. When that was gone, he pulled out a water bottle from the backpack and took a drink. Suddenly, he spoke, "I'm bored. Do you play checkers?"

"Uh, yes."

Pulling out a rolled-up checkers board and a box of checkers, the monkey quickly set up the game.

"Do you have a name?" Dimitri asked.

"Curious George," the monkey replied. "You can call me George."

Dimitri had the first move. Unbelieving but curious, he played. He was considered quite good; he beat all his crew and most other people he'd met. He quickly learned the monkey was *very* good. He struggled to get a tie but failed to prevent one of his simian opponent's checkers from becoming a king.

The next game, Dimitri managed to eke out a tie. George said, "Congratulations! Few can work a draw from me. Now, let me go first."

That was another loss.

They played several more games, with the same result: Dimitri could tie if he went first, but he lost if the monkey did. He couldn't help it; he felt proud he tied the monkey. It did help pass the time.

They arrived at their destination. Nothing was there.

"Now you must wait," George said.

The sun set, and the ship's running lights were the only illumination on the cloudy sea. Suddenly the intercom blared, "Ship off the port bow! No running lights!"

"That's what we're to meet," George said.

The dark ship stopped parallel to their ship. It was another container ship, but far larger.

"Order the crew to help transfer the cargo."

Feeling like a deckhand with a gun to his head, Dimitri glumly gave the orders.

The huge ship loomed over them as its crew transferred the containers from the *Stella Moru* with a crane.

When the unloading was complete, George said, "Now you."

Before he got on the transfer gondola, Dimitri said to his first mate, Kostos, "Take over. I don't expect to come back." Then Dimitri transferred over with George and the snake.

Looking down on his ship from the other, it seemed small compared to the looming mass of the mystery ship. He heard a strange sound, like compressed air released from an enclosed space, on his side of the deck, or slightly below. A splash followed, and then, quickly, a thunderous explosion— against the side of the *Stella Muro*.

"My ship!" Dimitri cried.

"You didn't think we'd leave any witnesses, did you?" George asked with genuine curiosity.

"My men! The waste of life! I should have died with her and my men. Why did you leave me alive?"

"Because you play a good game of checkers."

* * *

Vik Staskas noted the alert that flashed across his desk. Sam and Lisa had picked up the thumb drive he had planted in the truck. The virus he had placed in the file sent him a message that they had opened the file. He was mildly impressed. He thought there was only a slim chance they'd find the truck and the drive. They were pretty thorough. Too bad he was two steps ahead of them, leading them in the wrong direction. He chuckled as he reviewed their web searches from Lisa's laptop. They would be in Los Angeles tonight. Right where he wanted them.

* * *

Sam and Lisa arrived at Los Angeles airport three hours later. They'd taken a nap on the plane, but not before Sam got a report from the coast guard: they found the *Stella Moru*, or what was left of it. The ship had been torpedoed and sunk. Amazingly, the crew had escaped via a lifeboat—with eleven crew members on it. Another two had been found alive in the debris, along with six dead bodies. That left eleven unaccounted for, including the captain, Dimitri Koumundoros.

It was past midnight Central time, 10:00 p.m. Pacific, when Sam and Lisa got to the coast guard station at Long Beach port, where the *Stella Muro* survivors were being interviewed by the coast guard.

"We'll find them," Captain Griswold said, his mouth set in grim determination, after briefing Sam and Lisa.

"Why are you so sure?" Lisa asked.

"Ma'am, the crew reported a thousand-foot container ship sank them. Those don't just appear and disappear."

"I suppose not," Sam said. "Were there any identifying marks on the ship?"

"No, the whole ship was blacked out. They had spotlights trained on the *Stella Moru* during the cargo transfer, and the crew couldn't see anything."

The coast guard was nearly done interviewing the ship's survivors when Sam and Lisa arrived. The last to be interviewed was the first mate, Kostos Stavrinides.

"What can you tell us about the hijackers?" asked Lieutenant Larry Stockman, the coast guard intelligence officer.

"We never saw anyone."

"What did you see?"

"The ship drew near to us in the dark, blacked out. The captain ordered us to transfer our cargo."

"Why would he do that?"

"I think they were blackmailing him."

"Why do you say that?"

"He looked fearful. The only time I've seen him fearful in twelve years of sailing with him was when we nearly went down in a typhoon near China."

"What do you think frightened him?"

"It could only be his own death. When I saw him transferring to the pirate ship, he ordered me to take command. I think he thought he was not coming back."

"No other crew member mentioned the captain was still alive! Why not?"

"I was the only one with him. The others were transferring the cargo."

"What exactly did Captain Koumondoros say?"

"'Take command. I don't expect to come back.'"

"And you didn't see any crew on the other ship?"

"No, the spotlights made it impossible to see anything in the dark. But," he added, puzzled, "a monkey and a snake went with him to the ship."

"What! Were they his pets?"

"No, we had no pets on the ship. The monkey was small, with a tail. The snake was big, over ten feet long."

"What did it look like?"

"Kind of olive gray. It moved as fast as a man could walk. It was weird; it followed the monkey like it was a pet."

Quickly bringing up an internet search on his computer for *olive-gray snakes*, Lieutenant Stockman projected a screen of images on the room's display.

"This one?"

"No."

"Look down and see if you see one that matches."

Halfway down the page, Kostos pointed, "That one."

Expanding on the snake's picture, they all read *black mamba*.

"That's one of the world's most venomous snakes! It's also one of the fastest."

"That's the snake I saw."

"That explains his fear. But it doesn't explain the monkey or how they were used to hijack the ship. There must have been someone behind them."

"Could be. But that's all I know."

"Thank you. You've been a tremendous help."

"Glad to help." As he got up, Kostos paused and said, "If I can do anything to help, let me know. I want to get those bastards."

"Could I ask a question?" Lisa interjected.

"Sure," the intelligence officer said.

"Kostos, what was the captain doing before the hijacking?"

"He was in his cabin the whole time after we left the port. That was unusual. He also gave the order to turn hard to port, taking us off the shipping lanes."

"When was that?" the lieutenant asked quickly.

"About 1930."

"That's when the plan B said they would take over the ship!" Sam said.

"Plan B? That's right. The LA port authority said you had found some plans of the hijacking."

"I think the mamba was used to threaten him from the time you left the port!" Lisa said.

"Could be," the intelligence officer said. "I've never heard of a tame mamba. And what about the monkey?"

"There was something odd about the monkey," Kostos added. "He had a metal cap, like a yarmulke. And he had a backpack."

"A metal yarmulke? On a monkey?" Lieutenant Stockman wondered. "Let's see if we can identify the monkey. How much would you say it weighed?"

"Maybe five pounds."

The lieutenant brought up a screen full of long-tailed monkeys. Immediately Kostos pointed to the first image: "That one!"

"A capuchin monkey," read the officer.

"They're trainable. I've heard of them being used as service animals," Sam put in.

"Maybe it was trained to bring a radio on board. Then the hijackers used the mamba to threaten the captain."

"How did they control the mamba?" Lisa asked.

"Got me," Lieutenant Stockman said.

"We've got to get this story out!" Lisa said. "Can we use your network?"

"Normally, no," Captain Griswold said. "However, as a public service, I can let you have access if you let us scan your laptops for viruses."

"Let's do it!" Lisa got out the laptop. They connected it to a scanning station. After five minutes scanning, it was clean, as was Sam's.

Connected to the station's network and then to the internet, they prepared the stories. Sam wrote up the Manhattan story while Lisa wrote the ship hijacking. They added their video interviews. But when they tried to upload their stories, the network firewall stopped them.

"Let me open the firewall for your computer," Lieutenant Stockman said. "That's the *Midley Beacon* site and YouTube, right?"

"Yes," Sam said.

"Hmmm. There's another program trying to transmit. I wonder if this is an unknown virus? Let me get on your computer and disable it." He did so and took a copy of the program and then deleted it. He also found it on Sam's computer and deleted it.

They uploaded their stories.

"I'm worried about that virus," Lisa said.

"I'll send it to our security department. They'll figure it out, and I'll let you know. It's no longer on your computers."

By the time Lisa had published their stories and videos, it was nearly 2:00 a.m. Pacific time, 4:00 a.m. Central. Exhausted, Sam and Lisa retired to the closest motel and immediately fell asleep.

* * *

Dayton mayor Dorothy Burns settled behind her desk for another day. She studied her agenda on her computer screen, when another window popped up, filling her whole screen.

"Crappy pop-up ads," she grumbled. She clicked on the window to remove it, and it didn't respond.

A video of a man in a Guy Fawkes mask appeared.

"Hello, Mayor Burns."

"Who are you?"

"What matters is what will you do with a black mamba behind you?"

She turned her head and saw a black mamba perched on the back of her chair, inches from her face. Its black mouth opened wide and hissed. Fear choked her and prevented a scream.

"W-what do you want?"

"One billion dollars in Bitcoins by five p.m. today. I know you have ten million in your city account for the payroll, and the state of Ohio has the rest. Click on this link to transfer it to me."

She clicked and said with wonder, "That's PayPal!"

"That's right. It's the quickest way to move the money to me. I'll buy the Bitcoins."

After she had transferred the money, the anonymous figure said, "Now call your friend the governor and get him to transfer the money to the same link. I'll transmit the video of you and the black mamba to him. That should get him to move."

Her secretary, Jeff Washington, walked in. "Ms. Burns— there's a snake!" he yelled.

"Don't move or your mayor is dead!" threatened the masked figure on the computer screen. But Jeff had already run for security.

"He's gone."

"I know."

"Am I going to die?"

"Maybe."

Chapter 4

Dayton

At 7:00 a.m. LA time the next morning, Sam awoke to his cell phone playing "Livin' the Vida Loca." Groggily, Sam reached for it. It was the turkey hotline. Another zombie attack?

"Hello?" he said, sleepiness roughening his voice.

"Oh no!" Sam cried, instantly awake.

Lisa awoke to the sound of his voice and heard real dismay.

"What?"

"It's Lashon. Mambas and monkeys have taken over Dayton, Ohio. An anonymous hacker is threatening to kill all police and city officials if he doesn't get a billion dollars in Bitcoins."

"Let's go there and get the story!"

"I'll call Diane and get some zombie help."

Sam and Lisa raced to the Los Angeles airport, where they met Dan Cosana and took off for Dayton. At the same time, Diane took the zombie corgis, a flock of zombie turkeys, and six zombie bulls to a rented cargo plane at the Gary airport and also flew to Dayton.

* * *

As Sam and Lisa approached the airport, Dan Cosana said, "We can't land in Dayton."

"Why not?" Lisa demanded.

"The cyborg animals have taken over the airport. The last message I had from the air traffic controller is, 'Black mambas!'"

"That sucks."

"What's the closest airport to Dayton?" Sam asked.

"Um..." Dan scanned his 4G tablet. "Dayton–Wright Brothers Airport. No control tower. Ten miles away."

"Make it so, Number 1."

"Lisa, you're channeling Captain Picard again," Sam put in.

"Sam, call and get a rental car ready there. And a truck for Diane's zombie animals. Call Diane and tell her about the change in airports."

The rental car and truck were on the tarmac when they taxied to a stop.

"I see you've got a big SUV. You like your big cars, don't you?" Lisa said.

"Don't go to a zombie apocalypse without them!"

"We don't know they're zombies. Speaking of which, let's put on these Kevlar vests and helmets. That'll help against the mambas."

"I feel like a knight in armor," Sam said after putting them on.

"I've also packed these riot helmets, Kevlar gloves, and our trusty flamethrowers."

"We should be good to go!" Sam peeled rubber in the SUV, and off they raced.

Diane, after leading the turkeys, corgis, and bulls into the truck, followed them.

"Let's go to city hall first, then the police station," Lisa said to Sam and then called Diane to relay the plan to her.

They rushed into city hall and found a standoff. City employees perched on desks, plinths, and railings, just out of reach of menacing black mambas and rats.

"Don't come any further or the mayor gets it!" a rat said menacingly from the top of the mayor's desk.

The mayor, Dorothy Burns, standing on her desk, yelled as two black mambas began climbing it. She leapt to the rotating ceiling fan and clung on for dear life.

"I think we need some zombie help," Sam said.

"Right behind you!" Diane cried, followed by hundreds of turkeys, fifty corgis, and six angry bulls.

She dashed to the desk below the mayor, grabbed the mambas by their heads, and crushed them. Casually, she backhanded the rat into the wall. It smashed into a bloody disk like roadkill, splintering the dark wood paneling. Slowly, it slid to the ground.

Another rat appeared at the door. "Everyone dies now!" It sounded like a radio announcer from hell. Hundreds of mambas attacked the zombies. The deadly venom knocked out the turkeys and the corgis, but it had no effect upon the bulls, who roamed stomping rats and mambas with wild abandon.

Now the rats and mambas were the ones scurrying for higher ground. That helped them little when the corgis and turkeys awoke a minute later, as good as new and far angrier. The turkeys flew up and caught the mambas from above, pecking out their brains with delight. The corgis raged through city hall like land sharks, gobbling rats and mambas alike. Within minutes, the zombies cleaned the building of the deadly cyborg animals—although now it stunk of dung from the bulls.

"Sorry about the mess," Diane said. "They're not house broken."

"That's OK," said the mayor. "We're used to bullshit in city hall."

"Let's go to the police station next," Lisa said.

"Sounds good, but lemme leave some guard turkeys here in case they come back," Diane said. A dozen red-eyed turkeys remained behind, pecking at the mamba and rat bodies.

As they left, Sam asked Diane, "How did you assert dominance over that zombie bull?"

"I tore its head off."

"How could you do that!"

"I tore off each leg first. Inch by inch, it's a cinch!" she said cheerily.

Gunshots sounded from the police station as they approached.

"Sounds like a firefight. We'd better be careful," Sam said.

"'Careful' is not in our vocabulary!" yelled Diane as she, the turkeys, and the corgis charged in. She commanded the bulls to stay outside.

"Doesn't look like this is our fight, Lisa."

"Good. Snakes creep me out."

Inside the police station, the police barricaded themselves in various offices, away from the mambas. The rats chewed through walls, and the police shot them as they came through. The corgis followed the rats into the holes and killed mambas and rats alike. Any that fled into the hallways were killed by the turkeys. Any that escaped outside were killed by the bulls. Sam and Lisa flamed a few remaining scuttling snakes and rats.

Leaving the police station, Sam and Lisa saw marines landing in helicopters. They went house to house and block to block looking for rats and mambas. When they spotted the animals in the open, the marines fired fléchettes. The zombies accompanied them, getting up close and personal when people and cyborgs intermingled. Diane provided zombie fire support, directing her turkeys, corgis, and bulls as needed.

The battle raged for hours, but the tide had turned. By evening, no mambas or rats were left alive in Dayton.

Unfortunately, it was too late for the state of Ohio. A billion dollars had been transferred to the now canceled PayPal account, which had been emptied buying untraceable Bitcoins. Normally PayPal wouldn't transfer that much money so quickly, but an emergency phone call from the Ohio governor to the PayPal CEO circumvented their usual controls.

Military intelligence analyzed the cyborg animal corpses. They discovered the sophisticated telemetry and computer controls in each snake, rat, and monkey. Talking with Sam and Lisa the next day, marine Intelligence Officer Colonel Nguyen said, "These animals are actually cyborgs, remotely controlled. There is a computer in each one, receiving instructions remotely. This explains how the mamba and the monkey were controlled on the *Stella Moru*."

"Thank you, Colonel. I just got something from the coast guard IT department for you," Lisa said.

"What's that? I didn't know they had any evidence from the *Stella Moru*."

"It wasn't from the *Stella Moru*; it was a virus from our laptops. They found it was communicating with a server in Kansas."

"Excellent! I'll work with them and trace the server location. Then we'll hit it. We cannot allow domestic terrorism."

"This is really big. Could we cover the assault, as embedded reporters?"

"Yes. You've been a key help. But you'll be under complete military security and secrecy. Any stories must be cleared and released through us."

Lisa scowled. "That's not our usual protocol! I've never put up with censorship in my life!"

"I'm sorry, but we can't risk our soldiers, marines, and airmen's lives. You just can't tell which detail might give aid and comfort to the enemy."

"Stupid bureaucratic regulations! We're not going to jeopardize anyone's life!"

"We as officers are responsible for our men's lives. We are responsible for everything you publish. Any slips are on our heads."

"No! I'll eat a zombie turkey raw before I'll let myself be censored!"

"Hey, Lisa," Sam said.

"What?" she growled.

"Think of it as another editor. And we'll get access. No access, no story."

"Grrrr. I've never let anyone edit me before." She sighed. "But we'll agree in order to save lives. Do you think you can help clear our network of this virus? I assume whoever planted it did so on all our computers."

"Good idea. I'll send a specialist there to help."

"What about Diane Sydney and her trained zombies? Shouldn't they come too? They were a big help to the military in Dayton," Sam asked.

"You're right. We have to assume the hidden server location is protected by more cyborg animals." Hesitating, Nguyen said, "How much notice does she need? I'd just as soon not tell anyone about this operation until the last minute."

"She got ready for Dayton within two hours. I'd say that'd be enough notice for her. She never says no to any request for help."

"That sounds good. I'll contact her the day of our operation."

"Hmmm. They knew about SPEwZ Inc.'s zombie blood shipment," Lisa said. "Perhaps you should clear SPEwZ's computers too?"

"I'll order an IT security specialist there too," the colonel promised.

* * *

Vik Staskas swore. Between the coast guard and the lost cyborgs in the attack, the US military had identified the infection and cleaned their computers of his virus. Not only had he lost control of *Midley Beacon*'s computers, but SPEwZ Inc.'s computers had also been cleansed of his virus. He still had some control. Through his moles in the IT rooms, he could access their internal networks and email and keep track of their movements and plans.

Sam and Lisa and Diane were proving much more trouble than he expected. Their quick warning had prevented a clean getaway of his ship. He'd had to hide it in a cave on an unknown island off Baja, California. That prevented him getting the computer supplies to his manufacturing base on a Pacific Island he owned. In turn, that delayed the creation of many thousands more cyborg animals.

Then they had gotten to Dayton with Diane Sydney and her zombies far faster than they should have. He'd got his billion but lost almost all the cyborgs he'd allotted for the attack. Such was life. This would just be one more obstacle to overcome in his glorious career.

Vik studied his analysis of the *Midley Beacon*'s internal emails. No apparent plans turned up, but Sam and Lisa spent far too much time with the US military, whose security he had not yet penetrated. Their schedules were unusually clear for the next week. He felt they were working closely with the military, probably for a strike on his server in Kansas.

That was a hardened site, well defended, but he knew he couldn't stand a determined attack by the US forces. Should he bugout or fight? Slowly, a smile spread across his saturnine face. Why not both? Now, what would it take to get Sam, Lisa, and Diane out of the picture permanently? He thought of just the thing.

Even a zombie should fall before this cyborg.

Chapter 5

Manhattan

My Undead Mother-In-Law Blog—January 11, 2017, by Ron Yardley

"So this is what it means to be famous," I wrote in my blog. Ever since my mother-in-law burst out in all her gory zombieness, I'd been writing my blog faithfully, unburdening myself to the world. And along with my mother-in-law's fame, my blog grew in popularity. Now my blog burst into viral fame like a skyrocket. Over a million people subscribed to it, all interested in finding out about my undead mother-in-law and what it was like having the world's most famous zombie as a relative.

A mixture of pleasure and fear gripped me when I learned that the military found the cyborg hackers' virus on my computer too. Now I must sign in with an unmemorizable password (written handily on a sticky note on my monitor) and send a text message to myself just to post to this blog! But for a brief moment, I felt a little famous. Then I'd shudder to think of the hackers ruthlessly killing me like they did on the hijacked airplane and ship.

What should I blog about today? That was the eternal question for all bloggers. But for me, it wasn't the lack of subjects, but their hyperabundance. Shall I opine about zombies being banned from major-league sports? Naturally, their superstrength and superspeed gave them an advantage in every sport, so inevitably the NFL, NBA, MLB, and NHL banned them. So did the PGA. And professional tennis. And my own mother-in-law filed suit against each organization, claiming discrimination. Most pundits were sure she would lose. I myself thought she would. But she never thought she would lose. That alone made me doubt myself.

Maybe the zombies should have their own league, like the woman's baseball league in the forties and fifties. I could entitle the blog post, "A League of Their Own." There is nothing like paying the compliment of a little plagiarism. I'd footnote the title, alluding to the book and the movie; that'd cover any lawsuits.

I wondered if I should mention something good about zombies, for their fine work in guarding ships and planes against further hijackings? That didn't really fit with any segue I could think of. Oh, there it was: *For those who question zombies' right to have a league of their own, consider they already have one: defending against cyborg hijacking.*

There were my three hundred words. Should I mention zombies' successes in defeating the cyborgs' attempted hijackings? Everyone already knew about those. How about blogging about the controversy about them voting in the Chicago elections? Chicago already had a reputation for letting the dead vote; how could a few thousand zombies voting make it any worse? But that joke was three weeks old already. Zombies were politically pro-zombie, which cut across the Republican, Democrat, liberal, and conservative divides.

"Ron, how late are you going to stay up? Are you still writing about zombies in your blog?" Karen, in her nightgown, asked at the door to my study.

"Yeah. I've got enough for today. A famous blogger has to keep his audience happy." I submitted the blog entry. And so to bed.

* * *

Security clamped down on the *Midley Beacon*'s office activity. Every reporter and employee had to sign in with two-factor authorization every day. Every time an intrusion was attempted, the IT department changed all the passwords. All the email and disk drives were encrypted with still more passwords. And they weren't merely passwords—they were randomly generated, like "13B!c*&zei%3sSa@!4oq-?." Or they were passphrases, like "Lisa Melvin is a future Pulitzer Prize winner." Lisa thought of that one herself. Military security cleared it because they felt it was so unguessable.

IT support rep Phillip Gentian felt the whole thing was a pain in the neck. And that was just the work he had to do in resetting passwords every day. As the newest hired IT guy, he got the dirty, boring jobs. Far worse was the unrelenting pressure from the Boss to give him passwords every day. Even giving the Boss the network password didn't satisfy him. He wanted the passwords to Sam's and Lisa's computers every time they changed! The Boss told him to get a password manager for the *Midley Beacon* and give him access to that.

Phil felt he could have persuaded Sam and Lisa to buy the password manager. They were competent IT users and could see the practicality of it. Phil had already persuaded the other IT personnel to back the idea. But the military IT security liaison Sergeant Jenny Sylvester was adamantly against it. "A single point of failure" was what she'd called it. Sam and Lisa deferred to her.

Now the Boss had texted him, *Get the passwords or get fired.* Phil felt "fired" by the Boss meant dead. The hundred thousand a year the Boss paid him no longer seemed worth it. Maybe he could quit. Maybe he could get that zombie treatment. Better to be undead than dead.

TGIF, at least. A lot of times people were more relaxed on Fridays about security. He'd scope out the wastebaskets and desks for written passwords after work. That usually worked.

* * *

Sam and Lisa met daily each afternoon in a secure facility at the 182nd Airlift Wing of the Illinois National Guard at the Peoria International Airport to plan the coming assault on the hackers' server in Kansas. Working together under direction of the NSA, army, air force, marine and coast guard, intelligence identified the server's location as an abandoned missile site west of Manhattan, Kansas, left over from the Cold War. A series of shell corporations had bought it. The innermost organization was registered as a public charity: Kansas Veterans Benefits (KVB).

KVB collected donations over the phone and disbursed them to Kansas veterans. The charity and its volunteers were genuine, but the board of directors was obscure; no real people were behind it. The money coming in matched the money going out. The charity's headquarters and phone banks were on the missile site, given to them as a charitable donation from one of the shell corporations.

The actual server used by the hackers seemed to be one of the charity's, according to the internet registry ICANN. The military had done reconnaissance on the charity and determined that server was *not* on the premises.

The military determined the hackers' base was actually in the missile silo, designed to be impenetrable to nuclear bombs. The military, specifically the Air Force's Strategic Air Command (SAC), had keys and access to the locked and sealed entrance, but officials also assumed other locks or barriers safeguarded the entryway.

The Army Corps of Engineers had tunneled surreptitiously around the silo from three directions. They disguised their excavations as road work, a new fast-food building, and a well dug on an adjacent farm. These three points were where the main attack would originate. The army would use a remotely controlled robot to assault the official entrance at the surface of the silo. When the expected counterattack came, they would simultaneously blow three holes in the concrete surrounding the silo. Robots would lead the way, followed by marines with explosive munitions to destroy any cyborgs.

Sam and Lisa's role was strictly that of embedded reporters: recording the proceedings for posterity and subjecting their daily reports to official censoring, which still galled Lisa. She also suggested, "Have you consulted with Diane about using zombies as assault troops?"

"We're trying to keep this operation as secure as possible. We haven't involved Diane or SPEwZ in any planning. If we need them, we'll call them once the attack is underway," said Colonel Ramon Figeroa, Illinois's National Guard's former chief intelligence officer. His great work during the zombie turkey crisis led to his promotion as a full "bird" colonel, still within US Army intelligence. Sam and Lisa had worked with Colonel Figeroa during the zombie turkey apocalypse, and they trusted one another. Through him, along with Colonel Nguyen's recommendation, Lisa had been approved to have her and Sam embedded.

"Wouldn't it be better to have them on the site? Even by plane, it's two hours from Gary," Lisa reasoned.

"Hmmm." The colonel considered this. "Two hours' notice to Diane and her zombies wouldn't hurt."

"I wish you'd bend about the censorship."

"Now, Lisa...have we actually changed any of your stories to this point?"

"No. I just hate having someone looking over my shoulder!"

"It's just like you overseeing your reporters for the *Midley Beacon.*"

"But I'm in charge of that. You're not in charge of me."

"I'm in charge of the security for this operation. So that means I'm in charge of any publicity. So that means I'm in charge of your content."

"Grrr!"

With Lisa's angry acquiescence, they adjourned for the day. The assault would take place that Sunday when no one worked at the charity. No one outside the room knew the time.

* * *

Vik Staskas drummed his fingers on his rosewood desk on his yacht. He cruised the waters of the gulf while his US operations were underway. Just an ordinary hundred-and-seventy-yard superyacht, filled with a decadent, rich billionaire and his occasionally bikini-clad entourage. He made sure all the ladies were on deck as window dressing for any spy satellites or Google cameras. Nothing to see here, spies. Just move along.

He pondered when the inevitable attack would come. Not that it made any difference; his trap was set. It would spring when they attacked. He just enjoyed the game of trying to outguess the military. The obvious time would be Sunday, probably before dawn. But would they try to surprise him? Perhaps Saturday, just as the charity workers left after their half day of work? Before they left? Those times would be more unexpected.

He didn't anticipate any surprises, but he was prepared for them. And he had SPEwZ and the zombies and their families under twenty-four-hour surveillance. If they moved, he'd know something was afoot.

He'd accepted the security blackout at the *Midley Beacon* and SPEwZ offices. He didn't really intend to replace his IT spy at the *Midley Beacon;* he just liked using threats. People could be so creative under pressure. And he knew the tightest security could be pierced by one lax person.

* * *

Diane Newby's cell phone rang at 4:00 a.m. Sunday morning, playing her ringtone, "Music of the Night" from *Phantom of the Opera.* She'd always liked that song, and since she'd become a zombie, it seemed even more appropriate. One of the unfortunate effects of becoming a zombie was that her eyes became hypersensitive to light. The dark shades zombies wore in the day were not just to hide their red eyes but to protect them from daylight.

She'd shifted her schedule to sleep mostly during the day. A busy day and night tracking and conquering a flock of zombie turkeys in Wisconsin, followed by the long trip back to Gary, had exhausted even her zombie body.

She awoke completely and quickly and saw the call was from Lisa. They'd become close friends. This must be another zombie attack.

"Hello, Lisa."

"Hi, Diane. This is it!"

"What's that?"

"The military is attacking the cyborg hackers' base. They think they have everything under control, but I'm sure they'll need you before they're done."

"I'm on it! Our chartered cargo plane is on standby at the Gary airport. The corgis, turkeys, and bulls are there and in fine shape. Where to, O great zombie mistress?"

Lisa burst out laughing. "Oh, that's so like the time I called Sam 'the great turkey whisperer'! We're going to Kansas. Manhattan, Kansas."

"Ah! Is the base a half an hour away?" Diane remembered Lisa commenting about that after the plane hijacking.

"Even less. About twenty minutes west. It's an old missile silo."

"Cool! That should be fun! I'll call our pilot and get the zombie crew together. We've started calling ourselves 'Team Zombie.'"

"I love it! I'll have T-shirts and cups made up and sold on the *Midley Beacon* site. See you at the Manhattan airport."

They hung up. Diane bustled and got ready.

George awoke. "What's going on?"

"A call for Team Zombie. We're going to get a criminal mastermind."

"Do you need my help?"

"If you want to come. I'm sure this guy will pull out all stops: poisonous snakes, rats, monkeys, who knows what!"

"Sounds like fun. I've never been along on one of these zombie battles before." The Newbys left in their new blood-red Taurus.

A chipmunk at the base of their front steps watched them go in the gray winter dawn. It didn't know why it had to watch, but it felt compelled to do so. It didn't know its retina signals were transmitted to a missile silo in Kansas.

* * *

After private flights from Gary and Peoria respectively, Diane and Lisa hugged when they met at the Manhattan airport. Colonel Figeroa gave Diane, George, Lisa, and Sam a briefing on their way to their rental car—in Diane's case, a rental truck.

"We've got the place surrounded. They cannot leave. We've sent them messages to surrender. They've not responded. We will send the assault robots in the front door, the top entrance of the silo, as soon as you arrive. We expect a counterattack. When that occurs, we'll send in the assault robots in the side tunnels. We should have a complete tactical surprise.

"If the robots get bogged down, for whatever reason, we'll send in the marines, from the top and sides."

"And what is your 'if everything goes to hell' plan?" Lisa asked.

The colonel smiled. "We'll send in the zombies."

"That sounds like a song!" Diane said. She sang, "Send in the zombies. There ought to be zombies. Don't bother. They're here," to the tune of "Send in the Clowns," in a strong alto.

"Oh!" Sam groaned. "Diane, I know you're a zombie, but try to have some feeling for normal human beings. We don't regenerate our ears when they're wounded by singing."

"Sorry, Sam. I didn't know you were such a delicate snowflake!"

"Cut it out, you two," Lisa said brusquely. "This is no time for your goofiness. This is a serious life-and-death situation."

"Or life and life, in my case," Diane said softly.

They arrived at the silo. M1 Abrams tanks surrounded the building, as well as Humvees and Bradley fighting vehicles.

"Woah! You've got the heavies here!" Sam exclaimed.

"President Trump has authorized whatever it takes to take down this terrorist group," Colonel Figeroa replied. "We also have plenty of air cover."

"Launch assault robots!" Colonel Figeroa commanded. From behind the Abrams, six huge assault robots lumbered toward the main door of the missile silo.

The hydraulic waldo of the lead robot held the key to the Cold War fortress. It jammed the key in the aged, rusting lock in the top entrance of the silo, and turned it. The door opened. Floodlights mounted on the robotic heads filled the dark entrance with light as they clunked down the narrow stairway, metal feet clanking on metal steps.

The lead robot opened the inner blast door. As light shone in the dark room beyond, and the video screen of the remote-control operator showed a short, bowed figure clad in what appeared to be dwarven armor, with a shoulder-mounted rocket launcher. Even as the remote-control operator's finger pulled the Fire button on the twenty-five-millimeter cannon mounted on the robot, the missile launched hit the robot in the chest and blew it to smithereens.

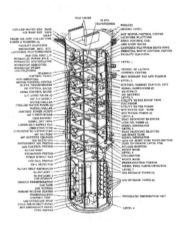

"We've got incoming!" shouted the robot operators.

"Launch the assault robots!" bellowed Colonel Figeroa.

From three sides, shaped explosives blew ten-foot holes in the silo structure, about a hundred feet down. Larger, more powerful robots moved onto the rubble-strewn floors. No floodlights were employed. Night-vision goggles transmitted an eerie green scene back to the operator room on the surface.

A rat scuttled by a doorway. Brapppp! The rapid-firing twenty-five-millimeter cannon in the chest of the robot obliterated it. A doorway across the room blew open, throwing shrapnel into the robot's torso. A Hellfire missile came from the smoking doorway at 30 percent faster than the speed of sound and hit one of the giant robots in the chest, taking it out of action. The other two robots in the room blasted the door with cannon fire.

Another door in the room exploded outward as they were firing. The robotic cannons swung to cover it, but close behind the shattered door came another supersonic missile, destroying another robot. From the first door, a small armored figure dispatched the last robot in the room with another missile.

"Crap on a stick!" yelled Brigadier General Harvey Walters inside the control room, a semitrailer in the parking lot. "That's a tenth of our attack robots down in the first wave."

"'When you're in a hole, stop digging,'" Colonel Figeroa quoted.

"You think we should abort the attack?" General Walters asked with a glare.

"No, I think we should hold our positions and analyze who's attacking us."

"I'm about ready to launch a deep penetration missile strike on this whole complex!"

"Yes, that would get it done, but we need to know who's behind this and where the cyborg animals are made to permanently solve this threat."

"You're right, Colonel," General Walters said with a sigh. "What can you tell us from the video so far?"

"The missiles are AGM-114 Hellfire missiles, available on the black market around the world. What's more interesting are the missile wielders." He projected a still image from a video onto the large screen.

It looked like a massively muscled dwarf in heavy armor. It held a Hellfire missile on its shoulder, pointed directly at the camera.

"The missile gives us an accurate measurement of its size. It's slightly less than four feet tall."

"That's crazy! Who would defend their site with dwarves?"

"I don't think they're dwarves. Look at this close up."

A circle around the creature's hand expanded to fill the whole screen. The back of the hand was covered by heavy black hair.

"Note the thumb. It isn't opposable. This is a chimpanzee."

"Who would give chimpanzees Hellfire missiles?" marveled the general.

"Someone who can control rats and mambas: the hackers."

"So this is how they'll fight us: with our own weaponry and disposable animal soldiers."

"I wonder how they control them?" Colonel Figeroa mused. "I'll send our signal and communication team around looking for radio signals."

"More importantly, how will we defeat them? I don't want to send more robots in there, let alone marines."

"Hi, everyone!" Diane called as she entered with Sam, Lisa, George, and a pack of a hundred corgis, cute and red eyed. "Team Zombie is here! Where's the enemy?"

They heard a large flock of turkeys gobbling outside the headquarters. The bellow of a bull also sounded through the door.

Using a schematic of the missile silo, with the three attack tunnels drawn in, the general reviewed the attack and the current tactical situation. "It'll be a tough nut to crack, even with unkillable zombies."

"No problem! The day we can't defeat chimps is the day I resign from SPEwZ and go back to church volunteer work!" Diane said. "Hmmm. We'll attack from the top down with the turkeys raining down on them. They can fly down the silo. Meanwhile, me and the corgis will split into three groups and attack following your robots. I'll send the corgis ahead. While they occupy the chimps, I'll attack from behind. That'll be the end—I promise you!"

"And if you get stuck, I'll help out," George said.

"I don't see what these corgis can do against these heavily armored chimps," the general said doubtfully.

"Have you ever seen a corgi, a non-zombie corgi, worry through a nylon bone? Their teeth are needle sharp. Now, these zombie corgis are twice as strong and twice as fast. The chimps don't have a chance."

"You're the zombie expert, Diane. God be with you!" The general made it sound like "good-bye and good luck."

"One more thing," Diane said. "I'm going to leave about a hundred turkeys and a dozen bulls on the surface, patrolling for any escapees. Don't let any of your soldiers or robots out there, or they will be attacked."

As the zombies trooped to their attack points, Lisa said to Colonel Figeroa, "Could we follow the attacks with your robots and watch what happens?"

"Excellent idea, Lisa," Figeroa said with a smile. "So good, I've already thought of that."

"And could we use the video on our *Midley Beacon* website?"

"We'll review it first, of course, but this silo is fifty years old. I doubt any military secrets will be leaked. So your answer is, probably."

Sam and Lisa settled in chairs before a bank of monitors. Three robots followed each attack group. Sam and Lisa recorded each robot's video stream to their digital cameras. They would edit the raw streams later.

The zombie turkeys launched first, from the surface. They burst through the silo doorway and were on the chimp before he knew what hit him. He struggled to reach his missile launcher but couldn't see it with dozens of turkeys pecking at the clear visor on his helmet. As he blindly groped toward it, his hands were pecked bloody and then reduced to the bare bone by savage turkeys, commanded by their Supreme Turkey Leader to attack all little people.

Another chimpanzee came in the back door and immediately launched a missile at the flock of turkeys. The fléchette rocket burst and shredded dozens of turkeys. The remaining turkeys overwhelmed this ape too. Soon both were comatose, bleeding to death from their unarmored wrists.

While the shredded turkeys slowly regenerated, the flock descended the silo, flying into every doorway and killing chimps as they were found. Meanwhile, the regenerated replaced those lost in each battle.

Then the corgis and Diane and George entered the silo from below. The corgis zoomed to the open doors where the chimp-mounted rockets were last seen. A storm of fléchettes came from each door. The corgis wore Kevlar vests, but still dozens of casualties decimated the pack.

"You've done it! You've made me mad! It's time to go medieval on your chimp butts!" Diane said.

In a single bound, Diane leapt thirty feet to the nearest door and jumped in. Two chimps were aiming at her with fléchette rockets from two angles for enfilading fire. Without hesitation, she sprang toward the nearest one. She hit it in its bowed legs while both rockets fired. The chimp she hit was knocked over on top of her. This provided her additional protection from the fléchettes. She had a Kevlar bodysuit and ceramic body armor on her torso and legs. A Kevlar helmet completed her defenses. Nonetheless, dozens of fléchettes pierced her.

Enraged, she screamed "No more subtlety!" and picked up the chimp atop her and threw it at the other. A two-hundred-pound chimp going thirty miles per hour made a substantial impact, even on an armored and powerful ape stronger than a man. The two fell tangled together like King Kong at the bottom of the Empire State Building.

"I'm not done with you!" Diane grabbed them by the necks and ripped off their helmets. One was completely unconscious and the other stunned. She slammed their heads together again and again until all she had were bloody stumps.

"Do you need any help, Diane?" George asked.

"Not yet. I have a feeling things will get tougher though."

Meanwhile, about half of the wounded corgis had regenerated and were at her side. "Up, boys! Let's meet the turkeys and clear out this joint."

Diane reversed the order of attack. She would go through new doorways first and draw the fire of any waiting enemy chimpanzee. She could dodge or avoid most of the fléchettes by surprise and speed. The corgis finished off any stunned or unconscious apes, leaving only bones in their wake.

They met the turkeys coming down the silo and then reversed their path, backtracking. In this way, they caught some chimps infiltrating behind them and quickly dispatched them. Now the turkeys went on ahead. They were more numerous and could better take losses. Diane followed behind her avian shock troops and knocked out any simians. The corgis cleaned up, licking up simian blood and gnawing flesh off bones.

At the bottom of the silo, Diane and George found a control room. One of the robots following them extended a mechanical hand with a key and opened it. The turkeys flew in, and flew out faster, hurled at unbelievable speed by whatever lurked in the control room. Fearless, Diane jumped in next and bounced off a huge Kevlar-and-composite armored figure. Six feet tall, with five hundred pounds of muscle, the adult silverback gorilla grabbed her. With uncouth strength, it grasped each of her arms and tore them off.

"Yow!" she yelled. She kicked him, getting away while screaming, "I'm not done with you! You're gonna get it," while her spouting blood quickly stopped and healing started.

"Let me take care of him, Diane?" quietly asked George, who had followed closely behind her.

"OK. I've gotta grow some new arms."

George was as armored as Diane. He and the gorilla were much the same height, but he was half its weight. *Being a zombie and more intelligent should help*, George thought as he hurled a heavy office desk at the simian. It casually batted it away with the back of its hand and then leapt upon George.

George fell back to the floor and kicked upward with both feet. The armored ape crashed through the suspended ceiling and then smashed into the cement ceiling above, leaving a gorilla-shaped hole.

Rather like a cartoon, George thought as the ape fell down. George grabbed a pole lamp and braced it against the floor, like a spear. It crumpled as if balsa, and the gorilla crashed into George's back.

The armored primate grabbed him, squeezing out all his breath. Bending over, George lifted the ape and ran full speed into the concrete wall. George heard some of the ape's ribs crack as three-eighths of a ton of combined bulk crashed into the wall. The gorilla's death squeeze lessened.

Just like playing football! George thought happily. While the ape was groggy from the blow, George grabbed the bowie knife at his belt and shoved it under the helmet and over the collar of the armor, up into the gorilla's brain. The ape became five hundred pounds of dead meat. To make sure, George cut off its head.

"Just like David and Goliath," he said aloud.

"David, my king!" Diane gushed as she hugged him, her arms bare and pink, newly regrown from their sockets.

A monitor blinked to life. A handsome man, with long blond hair and blue eyes, appeared. His muscular chest showed through his partially unbuttoned white shirt.

"Greetings, Newbys and the US Army! I am the master hacker you seek. You may call me the Master of Disaster! I send you this message not to congratulate you on defeating my cyborg army—I expected and planned for that—but to announce your defeat. Good-bye!"

An ominous rumbling began, such as one hears at a rocket launch. In the bottom of the missile silo, the metal floor dilated like the iris of an eye, revealing a cloud of smoke and steam and the tip of a rocket, slowly rising.

Stunned, the Newbys watched the monitor while in each other's arms. They were in this position when the rocket exhaust entered the room, filling it with flame.

* * *

The Master of Disaster continued the broadcast on military channels. The robot's video cut off when the wall of flame hit it from the rocket exhaust.

"I learned how to fight zombies from the *Midley Beacon*'s website. The fléchette rockets did a good job, as did my chimps and gorillas. It's not every day I defeat both the US military and 'intelligent' zombies." He made scare quotes with his fingers.

"I also got this rocket design off the internet, with a few additions of my own. Manned space flight is so interesting, isn't it?"

The image was shaking as the rocket accelerated into the stratosphere.

"No doubt you'll want to know where I'm going. It'll be somewhere on this earth, but you won't be able to track my reentry vehicle, which will be hidden from radar with advanced stealth technology."

"You won't get away with this!" General Walters yelled.

"But I am!" The Master of Disaster smiled. "Fifty thousand feet and climbing at two thousand miles per hour. Soon—"

The video flashed and cut off.

With a nasty chuckle, General Walters said, "Good shooting, flyboys."

"What happened?" Lisa cried.

"An antimissile missile, of a secret type. Hackers aren't the only ones with secrets. We thought the hackers might launch a missile, and had it prepared," Colonel Figeroa said.

"Send the robots through the silo. Search for survivors," General Walters ordered.

The robots meticulously searched every level, every nook and cranny of the facility, charred and burned beyond recognition. Still, half a dozen corgis survived, although piebald and scorched. Their hair and skin grew back. Several dozen turkeys had flown the coop—er, silo—and joined their fellows outside.

In the control room, where the rocket blast first hit, all that was left was the gorilla's composite armor and a slag of metal that might have been the control unit. No sign of Diane and George.

"Oh no," Lisa sobbed, clutching Sam. "This is the worst zombie disaster ever!"

"Yes," Sam said, "they lost more zombies than ever—at least since zombie turkey Thanksgiving. Yet out of their deaths, Diane and George secured a victory for our military."

"And more than that," Colonel Figeroa added.

For, outside, while the battle in the missile silo raged, the zombie turkeys and bulls roamed the square mile around the silo, looking for escapees. They found none, but they found a van with a large directional radio antenna. Without thinking or hesitation, the bulls rammed its front, sides, and back, completely disabling it. The zombie turkeys pecked madly at the windshield and windows, covering them in cracks.

Frantically, the men inside radioed the Boss. "Help, Boss! We're under attack!"

"Keep calm," he ordered. "I'll send help soon. Keep transmitting the signals from me to the silo."

"OK," they said, "but these turkeys will get through within minutes!" Already, the tough glass was flaking on the inside of the cracks, as the iron-hard beaks rained upon it.

"I've got it under control. Soon they'll all be destroyed. Keep transmitting!"

Meanwhile, in the Pentagon control room, the air force commander oversaw the launch of the antimissile missile against the hacker rocket.

A technical assistant said, "There's another missile launch, from the Gulf of Mexico!"

"Where is it headed?"

"The continental US, Kansas, near Manhattan—right where are our troops are attacking!"

"Blow it out of the sky! Launch immediately!"

"Antimissile underway," the assistant reported. "It'll be close," he added with concern.

"How close?"

"We'll hit it in one minute and thirty seconds."

"And how soon to impact?"

"One minute and fifty seconds."

"Start praying you're right."

Back at the communication van, the two men inside became more and more frantic, screaming at their boss to save them.

"Help, Boss! The turkeys' heads are coming through the windows!"

"Keep transmitting, right to death! Otherwise, your families will die—horribly!"

"Aieee!" They screamed in pure terror as a small hen worked its way through the broken glass.

"Keep trans—" The Boss cut off abruptly. The loss of communication with their omnipotent boss sent the two communication specialists over the edge into madness.

They fought and subdued the hen with their bare hands, but that didn't help them, as the windshield collapsed and the zombie turkeys filled the van. They did not see the spectacular flash in the sky as the Boss's ICBM exploded from the antimissile missile. Nor did the zombie turkeys; they were too busy feeding.

Later, the army corralled the bulls and turkeys and corgis back into their truck using the M1 Abrams, with Sam and Lisa urging the zombie animals, "Be good, little corgis! Come along, bulls! Come here, turkeys!"

The military found the van's telemetry to be a treasure trove. They discovered the encryption codes and methods used by the hackers. They also detected that the radio signals emerged from a computer center located in Scotland.

"It looks like we're going to Scotland, Sam," Lisa said.

"Road trip!" He smiled happily. It would be like yet another honeymoon for them.

"We have a problem," Colonel Figeroa said.

"What's that?" Sam asked.

"We won't have anyone to control the zombies."

"How about me?" Diane called, walking up

"And me," George added. They lacked their helmets. Their armor was charred and blackened. Their heads were pink skinned and the hair soft and short, as if it had just grown on a newborn baby.

"Whew! That was something," Diane said.

"Tell us all about it!" Lisa cried.

"When the blast hit us, it came from the control desk and pushed us into the hall. I grabbed Diane and carried her up the stairs and out into the surrounding area."

"While we regenerated our pieces and parts, we ate some nice roast zombie turkey!" Diane added.

"We're decent enough for the public now," George concluded.

Sam and Lisa hugged them and brought them up to date with what Colonel Figeroa discovered from the control van.

"It looks like we're going to Scotland next," Sam finished.

"I can hardly wait!" Diane gushed. "This is so much more fun than housework!"

"But, honey," protested George with a slow smile. "You just said the other day that housework was so easy now you didn't mind doing it."

"No, I don't," Diane said, smiling back into the shining red eyes of her husband. "But it's still not interesting, like getting caught in a rocket blast!"

* * *

Vik Staskas performed his postaction assessment. He'd done this since he was a street thief as a kid, reviewing his day, seeing what worked and what didn't.

Today was pretty good: he'd killed off a lot of zombies, including, possibly, Diane and George. He'd led the military and SPEwZ and the *Midley Beacon* to think they'd won a great victory and killed off the hacker leader.

On the distaff side, he'd lost a control truck before he'd been able to destroy it. He'd lined all his control vans with white phosphorus and placed a bomb in each. He'd never dreamt it would be taken *before* his escape rocket was destroyed. Those damned zombie turkeys somehow incapacitated his radio receiver! He took a deep breath. Calm. His error. He'd *assumed* they wouldn't be looking for a van a mile away. Wrong. Someone went looking, perhaps the military, perhaps SPEwZ. He'd *assumed* it would never be discovered while the operation was underway. Wrong. He sighed.

He didn't mind making false assumptions about the worst-case scenarios, but he hated making assumptions that only good things could happen. Ruthlessly, he reviewed the truly worst-case scenarios: First, they would decrypt his encoded signals. This was a sure bet. The US military was very good at cryptography. The obvious thing to do was to change his signals. That, of course, would signal them that he knew and some master controller was left. Far better to let them decrypt his signals, think they had the better of him, and strike back when they didn't expect.

He felt better already. The second scenario: They'd completely wipe out his Scotland data center. Again, this was almost a certainty, given what they knew and his desire to remain secret. His stomach clenched at the nauseating waste, but...there were casualties in war.

Third scenario: They'd connect his ship, *Rule Britannia*, to the control center. That would be *horrifying*. The ship was more than his main base; it was his *home*. He *must* prevent any connection between it and his crime empire. He'd have to go to Scotland in person, risk his life, and actually be present during their inevitable assault, controlling his cyborgs. It was risky, but the reward was worth the risk.

Finally, he smiled. He had solid plans. The reward would be complete control of the US, the crown jewel of his empire.

Chapter 6

Loch Lomond

My Undead Mother-In-law Blog—February 15, 2017, by Ron Yardley

"Hello, world!" I wrote in my blog. "My mother-in-law and father-in-law just called us up full of news about their latest zombie adventure. I know it's late at night, but I'm too excited to get to sleep, so I might as well tell you what they told me, while it's fresh in mind.

"This time Team Zombie went on an actual military assault on the cyborg hackers' base in Manhattan, Kansas. It was hidden in an old ICBM missile silo, of all things.

"After the hackers blew away the military's robots, the zombies went in. Not surprisingly, my mother-in-law kicked major butt. The surprise for me was that my father-in-law, George, participated. He hadn't been involved in any zombie animal battles. Knowing him as I do, he must have felt there was more danger this time and went to protect my mother-in-law, as unnecessary as that seems.

"It was necessary, this time. Mom lost both her arms to a five-hundred-pound cyborg gorilla. I saw Diane do half of that to Don. I'm amazed she survived. But that wasn't the worst.

"After George decapitated the gorilla, the Master of Disaster, as he called himself, took off in a rocket, and the blast scorched both Diane and George. They barely escaped alive. But the military took out the rocket, and the zombie animals captured a cyborg control truck.

"This 'Master of Disaster' seems to be a real character. He thought he was in control of everything—right up until his missile was blown out of the sky.

"You'll be reading about this in the major media today, but I thought I'd get out my personal version while it's still fresh in my mind. I think I can get to sleep now. Good night!"

* * *

Sam and Lisa slept soundly on the flight back to Peoria, then went home to Midley and slept some more.

Diane and George counted their zombie animal losses and also flew home to Gary.

Colonel Figeroa and General Walters planned and analyzed the intelligence they gathered. They decided upon two lines of investigation. First, they would direct their communication team to develop a means of interfering with the signals to the cyborg animals. That would stop any attack in its tracks, and it could be replicated on every ship and plane worldwide.

Secondly, they were able to capture undamaged control units from cyborg chimps. They sought to understand the protocols used to issue commands to the animals. The ultimate objective was to take over control of the animals, not merely interrupt the commands from the hackers.

* * *

When Lisa finally awoke, it was 8:00 a.m. "Yow! Sam! Wake up!" she yelled.

"Mmph?" he queried.

"We've got to get to work! We've got a million-dollar story in our cameras and on our computers, and we haven't published anything yet!

"Oh, OK," he mumbled sleepily.

Lisa had showered before she went to sleep. She was already getting dressed. "I'll grab a bagel and cream cheese on the way to work. See you there!" she said as she walked out the door.

Somewhat later, after a much heavier breakfast involving eggs and hamburgers, Sam walked into the Midley building.

"Hi, Sam," Lisa called from her office, breaking her own rule about "nonprofessional" behavior.

He entered.

"I've written the main story and uploaded the video of the attack—all that's been cleared by the military censors. That's about half of all the content we got in Kansas. Get in contact with the military, and get the rest of our video and interviews cleared."

"Will do!" he said cheerfully. Nothing like a solid ten hours sleep and a good meal to put him in a great mood.

* * *

Diane and George made it back to Gary with their cargo plane of zombie animals. They only had four hours of sleep, but that was a lot for zombies. They split a roast turkey between them, for a snack. That was not much for a pair of zombies. They'd eat more at lunch and dinner. They had to build up the reserves they'd used up when they regenerated all the skin they'd lost in the inferno in the missile silo, not to mention Diane's lost limbs and George's various broken bones. They looked emaciated.

Dr. Galloway had put them in touch with his colleagues at the Mayo Clinic when Diane volunteered to be a test subject of human zombiism. The clinic had discovered that the zombie bacteria, ECHZ, would transform from fat and muscle to whatever limb or organ was needed. Internal organs healed first, then skin, then muscle, and finally bone and teeth. With good fat and muscle reserves, a limb could grow back in fifteen minutes. When they were low on muscle and fat, it might take days for all the injuries or amputations to heal.

"You look positively skinny, George," Diane commented.

"And you look like you did in high school,"

She giggled. "Pretty close. I was down to one twenty when I weighed myself. I think I was one fifteen in high school."

"Did you read the story on the internet that they've started using zombie blood to fight the effects of aging?"

"Not surprising. Look how it's made us more youthful."

"There's still a lot of resistance to turning people into zombies."

"I can't imagine why. SPEwZ has been educating everyone about how zombies are just people like everyone else."

"The years of media stories portraying zombies as evil villains are hard to overcome."

"'We will overcome. We will overcome,'" Diane sang. Then she improvised: "We will overcome, or die trying! And then we'll rise to life, and then we'll rise to life, and then we'll rise to life, to overcome another da-ay!"

George smiled. Diane had spontaneously burst into song ever since their wedding. Her voice had gotten louder since she'd turned zombie. Their church choir director was quite pleased with the fullness it added to the choral sound.

"What are we going to do about all the zombie turkeys and corgis we've lost?" George asked.

"For the corgis, I'll go back to the Queen Elizabeth kennel in Hanna City and buy some more. We've lost fifty of our hundred. I'll buy a hundred corgis. I'm glad Heather Mallorn agreed to breed zombie corgis for me.

"For the turkeys, I'll go to Tom's Turkeys, where we got our flock. We lost more than four hundred. I'll buy a thousand. Hank and Betty Williams are breeding zombie turkeys exclusively for their zombie turkey sausage business."

"So you're still following the theory of 'get a bigger hammer if the first hammer doesn't work'?"

"Absolutely! If five hundred zombie animals don't take out the hackers, try a thousand! It's a good thing we have all the profits from our zombie blood sales to pay for them."

"We could have a lot more. You know we are selling well below what the market will bear. We can't keep up with the demand."

"So what? Do we need another million dollars? I'd rather help people and build up goodwill between men and zombies."

"I wonder when the attack on Scotland will take place?"

"I don't know, but I want to be ready as soon as possible. I want to get the bad guys!"

George smiled again. He loved his wife's innocence and gentle nature. Most people would call the hackers evil bastards.

* * *

Colonel Figeroa and General Walters, after working most of the night planning the analysis and research of the communication equipment and the attack on the base in Scotland, finally got to sleep on cots in offices in the Manhattan National Guard base.

When he awoke, the colonel immediately checked on the status of the cryptography research in the Pentagon. He felt his breakfast could wait, although his stomach disagreed.

In the video conference room, he talked with the head of cryptography, Dr. Susan Abel.

"Hi, Susan, what's the latest?" he asked when her thin face appeared.

"You've certainly given us an interesting puzzle." She sounded happy. "We broke it into three pieces: the encryption formula, the commands, and the brain-electronic controller interface. I'm pleased to report we've cracked their encryption."

"That was faster than I expected!"

"We've had over a million computers working on it. We crowdsourced it on the internet, without telling exactly what we were decrypting. We portrayed it as a contest, with the first one to decrypt it getting a cash prize of a million dollars."

She smiled, lighting up her pale-blond face. "It took less than twelve hours."

"Clever. Any chance of the hackers realizing this contest was their code?"

"Yes, there's a small chance. On the other hand, if they know we've captured their equipment, they've got to assume their code will be broken."

"True, but I think we got the head hacker."

"Or that is what he wants you to think."

"We did blow up the escape rocket. And it did seem that he was on it. But you're right—it could just be an elaborate ruse." He shook his head. "I don't like it, but I have to plan for that possibility. Thanks," he concluded with a wry smile. He made a mental note to analyze the messages from the rocket and make sure they came from there, not from some studio on earth.

"That's what we're here for," she said. "To solve problems and create others."

* * *

"Hi, Colonel Figeroa. This is Sam Melvin."

"Hi, Sam. Great job with the write-up on the *Midley Beacon*! You followed our guidelines very well."

"Thanks. What about the other video and interviews we have?"

"Yes, I got your material from Lisa and forwarded it on to our censors. I'll get them to send it to you today."

"Any decision on when we might go to Scotland?"

"No, I can't really talk about that over this unsecured line. However, you and Lisa stay ready. When we notify you, you'll only have a few hours to take off."

"Will do! We've got bugout bags prepared for just that situation. How about Diane and George?"

"We'll notify them too. They've proven themselves as reliable Americans. We trust them like we trust you and Lisa."

"I'll tell them to be ready."

"They seem to get ready pretty fast."

"Zombies are fast, despite the stereotypes of them as slow plodders. I'll wait to get the cleared stories."

"I'll have them sent as soon as possible."

"Thanks! See you in Scotland!"

"Bye."

* * *

Oddly, George and Diane were sleeping when the military courier arrived at their door at nine in the evening. They had been awake for nearly twenty-four hours, getting their new zombie corgis and turkeys ready for the trip to Scotland. They'd investigated the UK's importation laws, and zombies, including human zombies, were strictly forbidden. They'd purchased special contact lenses to hide their red eyes. They'd go as undeclared zombies. General Walters said the military would help with their undercover status.

The zombie turkeys and corgis were more difficult to disguise. They couldn't be anything other than what they were. Diane finally hit upon the plan of freezing them all. They could import the turkeys as frozen turkeys and the corgis as frozen pork loins. Opaque plastic wrappings covered zombie eyes, hair, and feathers.

As an experiment, she and George had frozen a corgi and a turkey using liquid nitrogen and then thawed them in cold water. They were good to go in two hours.

The courier knocked on their door. Even though they had only slept an hour or so, they both awoke instantly.

Diane answered the door. "Yes?"

"Message from Colonel Figeroa." He handed them a sealed envelope.

The colonel had decided upon a courier as the only truly secure method of communication for the launch of their operation.

"Thank you," Diane said, her bright-red eyes shining with excitement. "Would you like some coffee and cookies?"

"No, ma'am, I've gotta go."

She and George took their bags and went to the warehouse, where the zombies awaited in the freezer. They loaded their truck and went to the airport, where the shipping containers marked *Frozen Turkeys* and *Frozen Pork Loin* were loaded onto the cargo plane they rented. They flew with their zombies to Glasgow, Scotland.

They never noticed the chipmunk under their porch, waving good-bye to them.

* * *

Sam and Lisa met George and Diane coming out of customs in the Glasgow airport.

"Hi, you two! You ready to rock and roll?" Diane called to them.

"Like we always are," Sam replied.

"Do you have your car yet?" Lisa asked after she embraced Diane.

"Yes. We arranged for a lorry to take our 'frozen goods' to the rendezvous point by Loch Lomond. We'll take a rental car."

"How are you on the left-hand drive?"

"I've driven here before, on a business trip for GM," George said.

"I've never driven on the left side before," Sam said, "but I'm willing to give it a try."

"Let's go!" Diane cried.

The UK military had a base near Dunoon, Scotland, at Holy Loch, where they planned their assault. The base had originally been a US nuclear submarine base. That closed in 1992, and the US turned it over to the UK. It was a secure location for the couples and the military to meet for planning.

The actual hacker base seemed to be a bed-and-breakfast overlooking Loch Lomond—the Queen's Bed and Breakfast.

Military intelligence planned for Diane and George to stay there, investigating, while the British and US militaries prepared their assault based upon their reconnaissance at a sheep farm a few miles away. Sam and Lisa would follow the military's assault as embedded reporters.

The military communications corps traced the internet messages from the control van to the bed-and-breakfast's server, the same one that hosted the hacker's website. Military espionage had not been able to crack into the server or its router, which in itself was suspicious. The vast majority of commercial servers could be easily cracked by military hacking protocols.

George and Diane would prowl about the bed-and-breakfast, looking for the server. They would wear microphones at all times, with the top shirt buttons being video cameras. This way the military would know when to attack.

Colonel Figeroa, General Walters, and General Mackintosh of HMS Armed Forces sat with the couples in the briefing room at Dunoon.

After reviewing the plan with the couples, General Walters said, "I have extreme misgivings about involving you in this operation. You barely escaped alive in the last assault on a hacker base."

Colonel Figeroa added, "Further, we have no guarantee that the hacker doesn't know you're coming."

"As for me," General Mackintosh said, "I've never conducted a military operation with civilians before. Were it not for my American colleagues, I would not allow civilians into such danger."

"Don't tell me about danger!" Diane said. "I've had my arms torn off and been blasted by a rocket. I've been shot by a chimpanzee and bitten by a black mamba. I've been gored by a zombie bull and pecked within an inch of my undead life by zombie turkeys, not to mention nipped to pieces by zombie corgis. I'm not easy to scare."

After the planning session at Holy Loch, Diane and George drove their car to their zombie animals at the military's staging area at the northwest end of Loch Lomond, across from Ben Lomond. When they arrived, the military pumped water from Loch Lomond into the containers holding the frozen "pork loins" and frozen turkeys. Once the zombies thawed, Diane directed them to stay in their pens by the US and UK militaries' forward base until they were released. To Corporal Macgregor, who was in charge of them, she said, "Keep them well fed. If they get hungry, they'll migrate. The enclosure is really just a formality; it won't keep them in. Once you guys decide to attack, let them loose—they'll follow you."

Completely unassured, MacGregor agreed to keep the zombie animals well fed.

Then Diane and George checked into the Queens Bed and Breakfast that evening. After a dinner of roast lamb and canned vegetables, they openly explored the bed-and-breakfast's three floors of rooms; they were on the third floor. The ground floor had a reception desk and a small computer. Expressing a professional interest in computers as an accountant, George asked to examine it. Mr. Feeny, the innkeeper, readily agreed. George quickly saw it was just a retail terminal, not a server.

"Do you have any other computers here?" George asked casually.

"No, sir, that's all I can manage. I'm not very technically adept."

That night, after everyone had gone to sleep, George and Diane slipped out of their room and crept downstairs. They were dressed in their Kevlar armor and wore small radio headsets, complete with a video camera. This allowed the military to track their progress. They slipped into the basement and found the furnace, plumbing, a washer and dryer, a sump pump, and that was it.

"Hmmm," Diane said. "Let's prowl around outside."

They found an outbuilding with gardening tools and an old covered well. George separated the whole well cover from the well, bypassing the old rusty padlock. Diane climbed down a rusted iron ladder embedded to the stone. At the bottom, she found about ten feet of water and a drainpipe.

"Phew!" she said coming to the surface. Zombies couldn't drown but couldn't hold their breath as long as regular people due to their higher metabolism. Diane found holding her breath very uncomfortable. She'd once had her lungs fill with water, and while she didn't choke to death, she was uncontrollably driven to the surface to expel the water and breathe again. It had been her worst sensation since becoming a zombie. She'd rather have her arms ripped off. At least the pain subsided within seconds.

"Any luck?"

"Yeah, I didn't drown. I'm not as cold as I would be if I weren't a zombie. I can see in the dark a drainpipe that's too small to follow."

"Which direction does it go?"

"Away from the loch."

"That's uphill. So it's going into the well. From where?" he mused. "Hop up here, and let's head uphill and see what we can find."

Following the rough direction of the drainpipe, they climbed the side of the valley. Scrambling over the fragrant heather, Diane dried off, rolling in banks of the sweet-smelling wildflower. "This isn't so bad! Look at the view from up here." They were several hundred feet over the moonlit loch. The bed-and-breakfast looked like a small cottage below.

"We seem to be headed for that waterfall." A small spring of water poured out a rocky outcrop above them and cascaded down into the loch. With strong hands and great strength-to-weight ratio, the zombie couple had no trouble climbing the nearly vertical rock to the spring.

"My turn to get wet," George said. He stuck his head into the two-foot-wide tunnel from which the spring issued. "It'd be a tight fit for me," he commented. "It continues in straight as far as I can see."

"And I just got dry. Do you think this is some kind of underground entrance?"

"Straight tunnels aren't natural. But there's only one way to find out."

He started to climb in, but Diane said, "No, George, let me go first. If I have to fight mambas or rats, I'll have more room to maneuver than you would."

"OK."

Water filled about half of the two-foot tunnel. Gamely, Diane forged upstream. About twenty feet in, the tunnel split in a Y. A normal concrete drain went straight, while a smaller, natural tunnel filled with water merged from the side.

Diane turned to call George and saw him just behind her. He flashed a bright flashlight at the walls and studied them closely.

"This tunnel seems natural, but there are a lot of scrapes along it, like rocks and debris have been dragged out. I think when they constructed this drainpipe, they took the excavated rock out here."

"Do you think this is a drain from the hackers' server facility?"

"Or a drain from the road."

"There's no road along this ridge. The only road is by the shore of the loch."

"Let's see where it leads." George placed a wireless relay station behind them so they would not lose communication as they went farther into the cliff

Together they followed the pipe. Only a trickle of water was at the bottom. After a hundred yards, a vertical pipe intersected. Steel rungs led upward. The drain and its water continued onward, as far as they could see. Leaving another wireless relay station at the junction, George and Diane climbed the pipe.

The top ended in a sewer lid. George carefully, quietly, lifted it and looked around. "Looks like a basement."

"To what?"

"Let's check it out." Placing the lid aside, they examined the basement. Furnace, drainpipes, and a storage closet with tools were all that were there.

"Where are we?" Diane asked. She looked at the GPS map on her cell phone. According to it, they were near the top of the ridge above the bed-and-breakfast.

"This is certainly an underground facility," George commented. "There's nothing but bare rock at the top of that ridge."

"I wonder when the military will come on in."

"If it's only that waterfall entrance, it'll take them a while. I think they'll surround this area and look for other entrances."

* * *

"What's that?" Security Agent Stanley Smith asked his friend, Oliver Hardesty, as Stanley's security monitor flashed a red warning alert outside the server room.

"Intrusion Code 3060. I've never seen that before, not even during our monthly security tests."

"According to the security guide from the Boss, it's a breach in the basement drain."

"How did anyone get in there? I didn't even know the drain was monitored."

"You know the Boss is very thorough. Send the cyborgs to greet them."

"Bonzo and Alley Oop on the way!"

They watched the scene from the cyborgs' points of view using the cameras in their skull caps as they directed them toward the threat.

Following the Boss's standard practice, they stationed the cyborg chimps at right angles to the basement entrance to provide enfilading fire with their fléchette rockets. The Boss said fléchettes were the best way to attack zombies. Stanley hated to think they'd have to fight zombies. They were so creepy.

"Hold it right there!" Stanley shouted into his microphone as two figures emerged.

"Lie down and no one will get hurt," Oliver said.

The video cameras in the chimps' skulls clearly showed the woman looking to the big man and saying something, but the chimps' embedded microphones didn't pick it up.

The man said something inaudible in return, and then one jumped left and one jumped right, directly at the chimps.

Spasmodically, Stanley clutched the Fire button on his cyborg controller. The Boss found that gaming controllers were the best means of controlling and manipulating the cyborgs. All the security staff had used them before and practiced using cyborg video games adapted for training.

The woman leapt toward his chimp and dove below the rocket launcher before it fired. He jumped reflexively out of her way and chambered another rocket into the launcher. She flipped and bounced off the wall, coming back at his chimp even faster than before. Just as he fired the launcher, her hand knocked it away.

One arm clutched the chimp's leg, and the other tore the launcher out of its hand with amazing ease. Automatically, he hit her head with both armored fists. He could clearly hear the crack of her skull as it broke. He also heard another crack, even louder, as the chimp's leg broke as her arm squeezed it.

She went down on her knees, shaking her bloody head. He doubled his fists to break her back.

Just then Oliver yelled, "Crap!" He was bringing his fists down when the video monitor flashed and went black.

"Crap!" Stanley knew how tough that cyborg control unit was. They were tested with a sledgehammer before being installed in the chimp's skull. Glancing at Oliver's monitor, he saw it too was black.

"Send in Boris," Oliver said grimly.

"And Natasha," Stanley added.

"Can't hurt."

"Can't have too many cyborgs."

"Or too much power."

Per the standard attack protocol for using Boris and Natasha, Boris would occupy the intruders with a frontal assault and Natasha would attack from the back. Oliver guided Boris to the door of the next room, their cafeteria. Natasha lurked in the ceiling, ready to drop on them.

Glancing at the security monitors, he saw the trespassers hadn't left the storeroom yet. The woman was being helped to her feet. Her head was bloody but seemingly whole.

"Damn zombies," Oliver muttered. Stanley grunted in assent.

The zombies entered the cafeteria. Boris burst in on them, directed by Oliver. A lowland gorilla, he charged in his armor, arms spread wide, an eighteen-inch kukri in each hand, seemingly unstoppable.

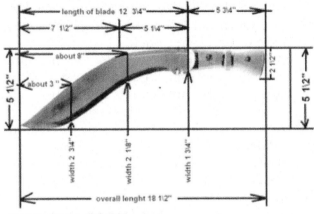

Dimension Sketch 1   K45 Kukri

One zombie charged for each cinderblock-like fist. Oliver jabbed at each as they came close. The woman dove under the fist, hit the bowed legs, and, incredibly, lifted the five-hundred-pound gorilla on her back. The man faked with one hand, then grabbed the gorilla's wrist with the other. A quick wrist lock and then a mighty pull, using his momentum and a push off by the woman, launched the gorilla toward the concrete wall.

Natasha crashed through the ceiling onto the woman. The thousand-pound Burmese python enveloped the small zombie woman. The man immediately pounced upon the python's head, but the crunching of the woman's bones could clearly be heard on the audio pickup.

Just as the man crushed the python's head in his embrace, the gorilla bounced off the wall and with a horrific double knife blow from its huge arms, sliced off the man's head. A shrill scream emitted from the python's coils as the small woman zombie jumped upon the gorilla's head. Her arms and ribs were obviously broken, but she still tried to choke the gorilla from behind.

"Now you've *really* got me angry!" Her shrill alto voice echoed from the speakers in the control room.

Oliver reached over the gorilla's shoulder with one long arm and grabbed her by the nape of the neck. She quickly broke one, two, three fingers, even as he hurled her into the wall. She bounced off like a rubber ball, shot across the room at an unexpected angle, and grabbed the kukri. In her small hand, it looked like a sword. She ran right at the gorilla, then dove to the side, slashing at the unarmored back of the calf, cutting the Achilles tendon.

The cyborg controller kept the pain down. Oliver had practiced with the gorilla in video game mode on one leg. He jumped and slammed the fists down. She unexpectedly rolled *toward* him, and he missed with both the knife and the fist. The knife sparked and bent on the concrete floor. Grabbing his right knee, she shot out from under him, slicing him in the hamstring.

"I'm bringing in Chuckles," Stanley said. Meanwhile, the evacuation alarms sounded. The data analysis team and IT crew fled through the pneumatic tube that was the only entrance to the facility.

Oliver noticed the Intrusion 3060 Alert flashing on his screen again. So someone else was entering the basement drain.

Frustrated, Oliver pursued the zombie woman, but she dodged and jumped about like a flea, bouncing off walls and slashing at the lightly armored knees and heels of the gorilla. Oliver couldn't believe he couldn't catch her. Boris's arm width was ten feet, and even with an injured leg, he moved quickly in the small room.

Then Chuckles entered: another gorilla, under Stanley's control. The cyborg apes quickly trapped her in a corner and moved in for the kill. She leapt straight up through the ceiling and started following Natasha's tunnel.

"Uh-oh. That's not good," Oliver said. The gorillas couldn't follow her there.

Dozens of furry forms burst in upon the gorillas. They bounced off the armored hides of the giant simians, but the bleeding leg of Boris attracted them. Dozens chewed at the exposed bloody flesh. Others tore at the ragged edge of the Kevlar suit. Soon the whole back of the leg had been stripped of armor. Then the front of the leg. The leg no longer worked.

Stanley guided Chuckles, who smashed and threw the fuzzy carnivores—they moved too fast for Oliver to identify them—as quickly as possible. Amazed, Stanley saw bare bone where Boris's leg had been. Dozens of the creatures were pulped and on the floor, but there must have been a hundred in the room. Boris also got some, but Oliver had him hop to the door to get away.

Then the birds entered. Large red-eyed birds, pecking and clawing with iron-hard beaks and spurs. Visibility disappeared as the apes smashed them and feathers filled the air, as well as the deadly avians and ravenous quadrupeds.

"I think we'd better evacuate!" Oliver said.

"I'm right behind you!"

The zombie woman dropped through the ceiling. Blood-covered, she had one red eye and one empty eye socket. Her broken arm had straightened out. She blocked their path to the emergency escape door and grinned at them like a maniac—or a deranged zombie.

"No more Mrs. Nice Zombie," she said. Then she whistled.

The ravenous animals savaging the gorillas came through the ceiling.

"They're corgis!" Stanley yelled. That was the last thing he or Oliver ever said.

With a grim smile, Diane said, "They're so cute." Grabbing her kukri, she whistled again for her pack. Obediently, they turned from their meal and reentered the cafeteria. "Let's see if there's anything left for you."

There wasn't.

* * *

Vik Staskas studied the wreckage of his Scotland base. That went about as well as could be expected. Of course, George would regenerate his head in another hour or so. Now for the coup de grace. His self-destruction signal could only be sent by him, from close proximity. It began with a video of his actor replica raving about destroying the base, sent to the military. The video ended with the actor theatrically pushing a red Self-Destruct button. Then the white phosphorus exploded in each room. After each room reached fifteen hundred degrees, a thermocouple set off explosive charges that collapsed each room under tons of rock. A swirl of smoke came from a newly formed crater on a ridge overlooking Loch Lomond, looking for all the world like the first volcano in Scotland.

Sighing with satisfaction at a job well done, he drove his rented Mini Cooper to his waiting submarine at the Firth of Clyde.

* * *

As soon as he realized the Master of Disaster guy planned to destroy the data center, General Walters broke radio silence and screamed "Get out of there!" into the transmitter. "It's gonna blow!"

The image from the video monitor on Diane's headset moved quickly, jerkily, from room to room. Corgis and turkeys followed in her wake. She bent and picked up her husband on her shoulder and then jogged down the stairs.

A blinding flash showed in the video. All communication was lost. A distant "Thump!" was heard through the heather-scented air, and then the observers felt a deep *thud* through their feet.

"Oh no," Colonel Figeroa cried.

General Mackintosh said, "Any chance they got out?"

"Look!" Colonel Figeroa pointed to a plume of smoke and fire rising from a new dip in the ridge above Loch Lomond.

"That's where they were," he said.

"Send some troops following their path through the tunnel by the spring," General Walters ordered.

After hours digging away rocks and broken concrete, the soldiers found Diane's and George's burned bodies beneath a pile of charred rubble in the sewer leading from the facility. Their skin was blackened, their body armor torn, and every bone in their bodies was broken, but amazingly, they were still alive.

Later, when they had healed, the military held their afteraction debriefing.

"Zombies lost?" General Mackintosh asked.

"Fifty-three corgis, two hundred and twenty-five turkeys," Diane reported. "The corgis and turkeys always bear the brunt of the losses."

"Are you and George totally healed now?" Colonel Figeroa asked.

"Never felt better!" Diane said. "But did we capture the master hacker?"

"That's the question," Colonel Figeroa said. "We captured their people as they fled the center. The patrolling turkeys and corgis found their entrance and surrounded them. I've never seen anyone so eager to surrender before. They told us how they were recruited and trained by their mysterious 'Boss.' They had only seen the video image of him, never in person. As far as they knew, this was the only remaining data center, after the Kansas one was lost. They mostly controlled the European operations but served as the backup to the US center, and vice versa. They had no idea where the manufacturing center was, nor their container ship."

"The bottom line is, we can't be sure we've hurt the hackers at all," General Walters said.

"Oh, we've hurt them some," General Mackintosh said. "They have one fewer data centers."

"We just have to assume they have others."

"How much of this story can we release?" Lisa asked.

"Just about all of it," Colonel Figeroa said. "If the hacker is still alive, he'll know what we've done. If he isn't, it doesn't matter."

"Would it be worthwhile going through the wreckage looking for clues?" Sam asked.

"We're already doing that," General Walters said. "We got to what's left of the control center using excavators and material handlers. It was a bitch getting them to the top of that ridge. All the electronics have been fused into slag."

"Not all," George said. He pulled a cyborg control unit out of his pack. Part of a chimp skull was still attached. He handed it over to Colonel Figeroa.

"Where'd you find this?!" Colonel Figeroa asked.

"I don't remember. I had some memory loss due to decapitation. But I found it in my equipment pouch after I came to."

"Another controller! And in better condition than the chimp ones you captured in Kansas! Good work, George!"

After conferring with the US and UK censors, Sam and Lisa released the story as a great victory in the UK. They showed the final video of the Master of Disaster and said he was "presumed dead."

As they flew back to the US together, Sam asked Lisa, "Do you think this is truly the end of the cyborg hackers?"

"I wouldn't bet on it. He already faked his death once."

On their cargo plane, with their remaining zombies, Diane asked George, "Will we see the Master of Disaster again?"

"Probably."

* * *

Vik Staskas moodily read the *Midley Beacon*'s report about the Loch Lomond raid. He'd accomplished nothing. He'd still failed to kill George and Diane or Sam and Lisa. He'd have to take more drastic action, regardless of the personal risks. The more personally involved he was, the greater his chances of success. And the more involved he was, the greater his chances of discovery. He never thought of failure.

Chapter 7

Midley

My Undead Mother-In-Law Blog—August 1, 2017, by Ron Yardley

"Finally, I think we're making progress in our family. The zombie portion of the family, that is. They've taken to wearing their colored contact lenses permanently. That takes out the yuck factor that everyone faces when they stare at those shining blood-red eyes. This also allows them to hide their identity to some extent.

"Diane is now 'out' as Diane Newby, and her whole family is known as the famed "zombie family" of my blog. Diane is the only one who is recognizable to the public, and only when in full zombie mode, with her battle dress. The rest try to maintain their privacy.

"With all of these special missions to control zombie animals and fight the cyborg menace, my mother-in-law's energy has been devoted to fighting evil criminals, not her zombie son and daughter-in-law. That's really good. We don't need another bloody intrafamily zombie fight.

"Then there's all this prosperity coming from the zombie blood sales. George got Diane to raise her prices a little: a hundred fifty bucks for one ampoule, instead of a hundred. She did that finally when the order backlog reached over a month. George convinced her when he documented that the government or the insurance companies were paying for over 90 percent of their sales.

"The 50 percent increase in profits allowed SPEwZ to expand their production facilities, to meet additional FDA regulations and security requirements, and left a little extra to move the family to a gated community where they have a little more privacy and security.

"For me, my dear blog fans, your faithful readership has permitted me to quit my job with Ion Marketing and go into independent internet consulting. The sales of the latest fashion in zombie sunglasses and contact lenses from this site also helps, as does the cooperative arrangement I have with the *Midley Beacon*, the world's foremost source of all things zombie.

"My mother-in-law's campaign for zombie acceptance is making headway, culturally speaking. They're now the latest rage on television and internet talk shows and TV sitcoms. Several zombie family comedy shows are starting, sponsored by HBO and Netflix.

"All in all, it's a sunny day on zombie street."

* * *

Captain Gerry Paulsen thanked Ron Yardley for the blog Gerry had read on the *Midley Beacon* for the tip about zombie eye-hiding contact lenses. He knew his new job with the airlines would be in jeopardy due to being a zombie if anyone knew he was one.

Oh sure, there were laws prohibiting discrimination against zombies, but all the airline had to do was say he had insufficient experience, and he would never have gotten hired.

He was also thankful to the Boss. He had been flying drugs out of Colombia to an airfield in New Mexico when the Feds caught them and raided the airfield. He got out just in time— to get riddled by a hail of bullets. He drove to the escape field, was picked up by the Boss's helicopter, and taken to the Boss's hospital. There, he had the choice of dying or being treated with zombie blood. The zombie blood did the trick.

The Boss, to thank him for his service, got him a job with a commercial airline. He also gave him a special chip under the skin in the back of his neck, which prevented any zombie rage attacks.

He was most grateful for that, even more than the contact lenses. As a pilot, he couldn't lose control and fly off the handle, like zombies were prone to do. He owed a lot to the Boss, but he hadn't asked anything of him.

He looked at the manifest for the cargo plane he was flying from Gary. Zombie blood for SPEwZ distribution in Texas. He smiled at the irony. Zombie blood flown by a zombie.

After takeoff, he circled to gain altitude and looked at the ground. He could see the new SPEwZ headquarters from here: a huge factory combined with a warehouse for gathering, extracting, and storing zombie blood, donated worldwide.

He felt a sudden urge to fly closer. He banked toward the headquarters. It had SPEwZ emblazoned on its roof in fifty-foot letters. They were advertising to pilots and passengers from the nearby airport, he guessed.

"Flight 5150, please return to your flight plan," the air traffic controller said over the radio.

"Roger, return to the flight plan," he replied automatically. But his hands nosed the plane downward toward the headquarters.

Horrified, he tried to pull the controls back with both hands. Nothing. It was like they were someone else's hands.

He screamed. Rather, he opened his mouth and nothing came out. The copilot was screaming and trying to gain control of the plane, but Gerry's hands locked out the copilot's controls, again without any direction from him.

In utter misery, he saw the 737's airspeed climb to six hundred, then seven hundred miles per hour as the giant SPEwZ sign filled his windscreen. The plane's nose zoomed toward the period on the *E*. Then, nothing.

* * *

"EEEEE!" Lisa screamed.

"WHAT?" shouted Sam, running into her office from his adjacent office in the *Midley Beacon* world headquarters.

"Sam!" she gasped. "A plane just crashed into the SPEwZ headquarters. A whole block of Gary is up in flames!"

"Oh no! Were Diane and George there?"

"They usually are," she sobbed.

"Do you want to go up there and investigate—or send someone else?"

"I don't know!" Lisa cried harder than Sam had ever seen her cry before. He knew she and Diane had gotten close, but this was like family-level grief. She had never been indecisive before.

"I'll call Lashon and have her investigate," he said gently.

"Th-thanks, Sam."

In his office next to Lisa's, he looked out the second-story window of their new headquarters. They had completely remodeled their old building and more than doubled their space.

"Hi, Lashon."

"Hi, Sam. Are you calling about the airplane crash in Gary?"

"Yes, please go there as quickly as you can and find out if George and Diane Newby have survived. It doesn't look good for them or SPEwZ."

"Oh, that's terrible. I'll get right there!"

In turmoil, Sam looked out at Midley Main Street. He enjoyed the view, after so many years of being at ground level. It didn't soothe him now. Midley Main Street was also County Route 15. Neither got much traffic. The main source now was cars going to and from the *Midley Beacon.*

A gasoline tanker truck pulled up and parked across the street. That was odd. The one gas station was outside of town. Maybe it had a breakdown. The driver got out and walked away quickly. Maybe he was going to the garage.

Then a ball of flame replaced the gas truck. Incandescent light and heat hit the windows of the *Midley Beacon* and blew them in as easily as if they were soap bubbles. The force of the explosion threw Sam out of his office and into the main reporting cubicles. That was the only thing that saved him from instant death as the whole second floor filled with flame.

Lisa too, though sitting, was also thrown out of her office by the force of the explosion. Ironically, they landed side by side, comatose, as the top half of the room burned at over a thousand degrees.

The bottom floor fared worse. In direct line with the explosion, everyone in it died instantly. But the survivors from the second floor envied their quick deaths. For those on the second floor were baked alive.

When the Midley Volunteer Fire Department had gotten the blaze under control and went through the floors, the dozen or so survivors had burns on over ninety percent of their bodies. Sam and Lisa were among those life-flighted to the burn unit at the OSF St. Francis Hospital in Peoria.

In the emergency room, the burn doctors performed a quick triage on the survivors. Six had a decent chance of living, although they would require extensive skin grafts and years of therapy. Four had a slim chance of living; they required 100 percent skin grafts. Three had no chance; the doctors prescribed morphine until they passed, to alleviate their suffering.

Sam and Lisa were in the last group.

* * *

Lashon circled the block of flame in Gary, where the SPEwZ world headquarters had stood. She had been there when the new building had been dedicated just a month before. That had been a nice, positive zombie story. George and Diane, Don and Maggie had all been there beaming. The single block held both the nonprofit SPEwZ charity and SPEwZ Inc., the for-profit firm that sold zombie blood worldwide. SPEwZ Inc. was the most trusted and largest zombie blood purveyor in the world. They had very little competition. Several firms tried to enter the business, but they could not beat the combination of low prices and high quality and guarantee of zombification.

Zombification had become an accepted and highly successful means of treatment for all kinds of formerly incurable diseases. Even chronic conditions like heart disease, obesity, and diabetes fell before the irresistible human zombie bacteria. Old age and Alzheimer's also were reversed successfully using zombie blood. People could be cured of their zombie condition afterward with antibiotics. But a majority of people felt so good in their zombie states that they refused the antibiotic. Thus the number of zombies steadily grew.

This was where the SPEwZ charity came in. They helped people get used to their zombie existences. They also collected zombie blood donations and paid a premium for zombie blood. They then sold the blood to SPEwZ Inc. for just enough money to cover their expenses. SPEwZ Inc. was a cash cow. It had revived the whole Gary inner city.

Lashon drove through a former slum where she had grown up that was now a nice middle-class neighborhood, serving the new zombie blood industry, centered in Gary.

All of that was up in flames. The 737 had been fully loaded with fuel when it crashed, vaporizing the fuel and generating a fuel-air explosion. That, in turn, ignited the whole fragmented block of buildings.

Lashon had a sick feeling in the pit of her stomach that all was lost: the zombie blood industry, the Newbys, and Gary's newfound prosperity. She talked to the fire department about once an hour for an update and then uploaded it to the *Midley* server from her *Midley Beacon* car, equipped with wireless internet connection. Oddly, the *Midley* server was down. She had to load the video to their YouTube site manually, which was still working.

She tried calling Lisa and Sam and couldn't reach either. Neither the 1-800-Z-TURKEY hotline nor the IT help desk could be reached either. The latter's inaccessibility was not unusual, but the rest seemed highly suspicious.

She called fellow *Midley* reporter Charlie Gomez. "Hey, Charlie, have you been able to reach anyone at the *Midley Beacon*?"

"You haven't heard?" he said, incredulous.

"Heard what?"

"The whole *Midley Beacon* building has burned down due to a gasoline truck explosion."

She couldn't talk. Or scream. Finally, hesitantly, she asked, "Any casualties?"

"Twenty-seven dead, thirteen in critical condition."

"Sam and Lisa?"

"In critical condition at OSF St. Francis."

Finally, she began crying.

As if in sympathizing grief, the skies opened up and poured rain. The rain helped cool the fiery block better than the fire trucks could. That evening, Lashon followed the firemen as they searched the wreckage for bodies.

"You don't have to do this, ma'am," said one concerned fireman.

"I have to. These were my friends."

"I understand."

The grisly search through the sticky wet ash found few bodies, and those that were found were charred beyond recognition. The firemen collected these in body bags for dental and DNA identification.

Lashon felt worse than ever but somehow couldn't cry. She couldn't feel. She wandered Gary and finally slipped into her old church and prayed.

* * *

Meanwhile, Lisa and Sam lingered in a coma for a day in the hospital, until their deaths, late one night, with Sam's father, Abner Melvin, present. Sam's relatives came and took the bodies home, where they had a quiet and private burial on Abner's farm, side by side.

Lashon and her husband, Rulon, attended the closed-casket ceremony. Lashon wept as she watched the caskets lowered into the flower-covered grass in the private cemetery. This was the end of one phase of her life. She would carry her memories of Sam and Lisa with her forever.

* * *

My Undead Mother-In-Law—August 9, 2017, by Ron Yardley

"I don't want to write this blog. I also didn't want my mother-in-law, father-in-law, brother-in-law, and sister-in-law to die. We don't always get what we want. We don't always get to do what we want. Life—and death—happens to us, and we have to deal with it. Even me.

"I've put it off all day. I'm exhausted and need to sleep. But I can't until I write this.

"Today we held a memorial service for my deceased family: George, Diane, Don, and Maggie Newby, as well as the rest of the SPEwZ employees killed in the terrorist attack. The fire department and construction-worker volunteers had been working all week looking for bodies. They found only a few remains of the more than fifty employees who worked at SPEwZ charity and SPEwZ Inc.

"The volunteers were thorough and had worked tirelessly. Many were zombies saved from death and disability by zombie blood from SPEwZ. Many worked continuously, twenty-four hours a day, all week—until there was nothing more to do. The whole block had been excavated to the foundations. All the rubble had been sifted and shipped away. The girders and bricks had been removed. No more bodies were to be found.

"There were still hundreds and thousands of body parts to be identified. No DNA samples matched my relatives yet. But that was moot. All that was left was ash.

"And that's what I have left in my heart—ash. No feelings, cold and lifeless.

"Yet a flower springs in the ash. My wife, Karen, still loves me. She told me she was pregnant. If it's a girl, we'll name her Diane."

* * *

The zombie blood industry was completely disrupted. SPEwZ had processed and sold over 90 percent of all zombie blood worldwide. Gary put in for Federal Disaster relief and got it. FEMA arrived soon afterward.

One small, weak competitor in the zombie blood industry quickly rose above the others: E-Z Cure. They guaranteed the same quality as SPEwZ Inc. and the same prices, for both buying and selling the blood. They too were a storefront operation, like SPEwZ used to be. Based in Houston, Texas, they took advantage of the favorable state tax laws and a large number of zombies in Texas to jump start their business.

E-Z Cure grew exponentially after the demise of SPEwZ Inc. As they grew, to fund their expansion, they charged 100 percent markup for shipping and handling. People who were dying didn't care. The insurance companies vetted the cost of the blood but not the cost of the shipping.

E-Z Cure had a single, wealthy founder, who bankrolled their expansion in exchange for complete ownership and control: a certain D. Masters. Tall, handsome, and with long blond hair, he looked more like a surfer left over from the sixties than a businessman. But he talked the talk and funded their growth until the day E-Z Cure went public on the NY Stock Exchange, six months after the Gary disaster.

Mr. Masters doubled his money, then doubled it again. He sold enough of his stock to be a billionaire but still retained control of the corporation. During the six months of growth, he introduced several new products, notably, a computer chip guaranteed to prevent zombie symptoms, such as uncontrollable rage. The chip would be implanted under the skin at the back of the neck, like a tracking chip on dogs. They also sold contact lenses to hide zombies' eyes. Becoming a zombie had never been so easy or convenient.

However, once they dominated the market like SPEwZ did, their prices slowly rose for everything. The demand did not slacken. Everyone wanted to be cured of their diabetes, or Alzheimer's, old age, or cancer. Even lost limbs and eyesight were cured by zombie blood. The costs were covered by insurance or Medicaid or Medicare.

Culturally, the country completely accepted zombies. Diane Newby's goals had been achieved posthumously. Zombies were in the military and in the government. Senators and representatives, federal and state judges were zombies, as well as members of President Trump's cabinet and the president's chief of staff.

The majority of the new zombies used the implanted chip. There were no incidents of human zombies going out of control and no claims on E-Z Cure's ironclad guarantee.

Amazingly, the *Midley Beacon* came back. Their insurance policy rebuilt the building, the web servers, and the printing press. The surviving reporters rallied together to restart the paper, and Mr. Masters, of E-Z Cure, generously donated funds to get the paper started again. A lot of the content had been stored online in cloud backup, so their web presence had not been lost. Charlie Gomez and Lashon Miller, as senior reporters, became head editors. Mr. Masters kindly supplied Vasily Badenov, a Harvard MBA, to run the financial and operations side of the business.

* * *

Once Sam and Lisa were buried, and the SPEwZ memorial service completed, Vik Staskas threw a party for all his employees worldwide. His victories over SPEwZ's zombies and the pesky *Midley Beacon* were totally satisfactory. He ran both the zombie blood industry, through D. Masters, his actor Master of Disaster, and the *Midley Beacon* through his agent Vasily Badenov. Both were secret cyborgs under his complete control. His only regret was that he lost his IT agent in Midley. He smiled. Now he controlled the CEO of SPEwZ and CFO of the *Midley Beacon*. It was a good trade.

With ownership of the *Midley Beacon*, he manipulated the perception and influence of zombies. Mostly. There were still hundreds of nuts and conspiracy theories out there, some of which were actually close to the truth. How he hated the free press!

As a byproduct of defeating his enemies, he gained zombie agents in the executive, judicial, and legislative portions of the US government through his zombies placed in key positions. The US was far harder to control than Europe. People weren't compliant to government edicts, and the US Federalism meant he had to take control of not just the federal government but each of the fifty state governments. Trying to manipulate and control thousands of zombies exhausted him. He couldn't lounge on his superyacht anymore with his bikini girls. He had to work seventy to eighty hours per week controlling his zombie government officials from his underground fortress near Manhattan, Kansas.

Again, he smiled to himself. He didn't like his underground fortress as much as his superyacht, but he loved the fact the US government destroyed the missile silo and never saw his fortress hidden under it. There was nothing better than letting your enemy beat you and think they won, never to look again for your headquarters there.

The US was his big problem now. Even worse than US Federalism was the Constitution! It was specifically designed to maximize liberty and prevent dictatorships. Philosophically, he said to himself, "The reward for success is more problems." He eagerly began planning how to subvert the Constitution.

Once he had complete control over the US, the rest of the world would fall into his lap like a ripe fruit. It was his inevitable destiny, he realized, as he analyzed his life's trajectory from street thief to the present conquest and control of the United States, and into the future.

Chapter 8

Gary

Unobserved, in the pouring rain of the second day of downpour in Gary, Indiana, following the disastrous plane crash, a puddle of wet ash bubbled and then arose. Covered in black slime, a lurching, awkward form emerged from under the ash.

It soon discovered why the pit had not been touched or searched by the firemen and Lashon Miller the day before: the pit was covered by crisscrossing, warped, and twisted girders from the industrial roof.

Putting its shoulder under a girder, the form pushed. The whole pile groaned but did not move. Like playing a game of gigantic jackstraws, it tried a different girder. This one moved. It wriggled through the remaining girders like a black worm. Slime and burnt clothing scraped off. Once in the roofless pit, the downpour cleansed the last slime and charred clothing away, revealing a slender, almost emaciated man with glowing red eyes.

Free now, he paused. Although consumed with an incredible, burning hunger for food, he needed something else. His mind was fuzzy, dazed. Who was he? How did he get here? He was a football player—George! George Newby! But football was many years ago. He'd married Diane Sydney after high school. Whatever happened to her?

Like a lost man retracing his steps, he followed his memories. After they married, he went to college. He became an accountant. He got a job with GM after college. He and Diane had kids: Karen and Donald. Where were they? Where was Diane?

Patiently, doggedly, as was his nature, he remembered buying a house in Gary, sending the kids to school and college, getting promoted. And then—he turned zombie! "Ah! That's it! I'm a zombie! So are Diane, and Donald, and Donald's wife, Maggie!"

So where were they? Obviously, some disaster had happened to the SPEwZ building—he couldn't remember what or where he had been. He wandered the ruins, calling out, "Diane! Donald! Maggie!" over and over.

It took a long time to cover the whole block. He was not discouraged by the echoing silence or by his ravaging hunger. Finally, he got an answer.

"Dad?" A weak, high voice came from a pile of bricks. He vigorously dug through the bricks and picked up his daughter-in-law, Maggie. Plump no longer, she was a scarecrow of a skeleton.

"Dad, I'm so hungry. Do you have some food?"

Frowning, he concentrated on this problem. He was naked. She was naked. They were close to their home, but he'd lost his car keys with his clothing. He also needed to find Diane and Donald.

"Honey? George, is that you?" came a call from behind him.

His moon goddess, as he privately called Diane, came to him in the pouring rain, lovely as ever, although even thinner than she had been in high school.

"Diane!" He embraced her. "Now all we have to do is find Donald."

"Donny? He was right beside me when the wall collapsed on us."

"You remember? My earliest memory is going to work this morning. Everything else is a blank."

They returned to the pile of bricks, and Diane and George dug. Maggie was too weak, but all called, "Don! Donnie! Donald!"

A groan emitted from the bottom of the pile. Under the bricks, under a girder was Don Newby. He too looked like a concentration-camp escapee and was weak, but he managed to walk and help carry Maggie.

The four walked first to the parking garage across the street, unobserved in the dark, rainy night.

"I have a key hidden on my car," Maggie said. "I'm always losing my keys."

They filed into Maggie's car, and she drove to the Newbys' home. There they all ate four huge steak filets from the fridge. They didn't bother cooking them. For the second course, they planned a whole chicken apiece. The four chickens roasted in the oven while they gobbled the steaks. Afterward, the couples cleaned up and got dressed.

They finally laughed at how poorly their clothing hung on them. Diane had some of Don's old clothing at the house: a DOTA T-shirt, jeans, underwear, socks. The shirt hung on him like a Shar-Pei's skin.

George's clothing fit like it was two sizes too big. Diane felt she could get into her old size 4 clothing she wore in high school. She'd sentimentally kept her prom dress from thirty years ago and tried it on. It was way too loose.

"Oh, I can't wear this!" She laughed.

"For me, you can," George said.

Maggie wore some of Diane's clothing—sweatshirts and pants that hid her emaciated figure.

Now dressed, they finished clearing out the Newbys' commercial-sized refrigerator. They each topped off all that protein with their food of choice: George ate a whole family-sized pizza, as did Don. By the time the pizza delivery arrived, they looked quite normal, for zombies. Diane ate an entire cheesecake—the last survivor from their fridge. And Maggie devoured a whole box of sugared flakes. They had never been so ravenous—and they had never been so close to death.

Oddly, the *Midley Beacon* website was down, but the other news sites and the Midley YouTube channel made it clear what had happened.

"Grrr! It's that Master of Disaster!" Diane growled.

"I'm sure you're right, Diane," George said. "We need a council of war."

"It's pretty simple: find him and kill him!" Diane's red eyes glowed with rage.

"We've already tried that and apparently succeeded twice. Only he struck back, harder than ever. So we must change our tactics."

"What's your plan, Dad?" Don asked.

"Sun Tsu says when the enemy thinks you're weak, that is when you strike. Everyone will think we're dead. So let's maintain that and see if we can find this Disaster, this hacker, and attack him when he thinks we're dead."

"Good idea, George! Now, what do we have for money? Dead people can't use credits cards or checks."

"I have a couple hundred in cash."

"I do too!" Diane said.

"We have some cash at our house," Don said. "But not a lot."

"That won't last long. What other resources do we have?"

"Maggie's car."

"And our cars. If we get them tonight from the parking lot, people probably won't notice they've been moved. What about our friends?"

"I have friends in SPEwZ—oh no, most of them that aren't zombies are dead!" Diane started crying.

"When we go back for our cars, we can look for the other zombies that survived. Who else can we trust?"

"Sam and Lisa."

"Yes, let's get ahold of them first thing tomorrow morning."

"Oh no!" Maggie cried as she peered at her in-laws' computer.

"What's wrong?" Don asked.

"Sam and Lisa! They're in critical condition in the hospital!"

"What happened?" gasped Diane.

"There was a gasoline truck explosion outside the *Midley Beacon.*"

"The Master of Disaster!" Diane yelled.

"Don't jump to conclusions, Diane."

"I swear I'll turn him into a zombie before I kill him!"

"Why is that?" George asked, puzzled.

"So I can kill him over and over and over!"

"Dad, Mom is right. That's the most reasonable probability," Don said.

"Yeah, I know. I just don't want to make any mistakes based on a false assumption."

"It doesn't really change anything," Maggie said. "We still should get to them tomorrow, to see if we can help."

"No, we should go there tonight," George said.

"Why?" Maggie asked.

"Because we *can* help. We have zombie blood."

"Yes! Let's go now!" Diane yelled, flourishing an ampoule.

"First, we have to get our cars," George said.

"Then we go," Don finished.

They packed Maggie's car and headed back to the unaffected parking deck across from the ruined SPEwZ headquarters. Diane and George picked up their car, repacked the cargo, and took off for Peoria.

Don and Maggie remained behind, searching the ruins of SPEwZ for other zombies. They found some of their friends under rubble and in pools of water. Don and Maggie brought them to their home and fed them. They shared their plans for secrecy and counterattack. They all pooled their resources. Don and Maggie left as quickly as possible after feeding the survivors. The survivors stayed, agreeing to keep the Newbys' existence a secret, as well as their own.

Don and Maggie drove to the Peoria hospital to meet up with George and Diane. Don did a good impersonation of a race-car driver down I-55. No one passed him.

Meanwhile, George strictly followed the speed limit. But Diane didn't. "This is life and death, George. Let me drive."

"Hey, if we get stopped, it comes out of your money!" They both laughed at the old joke between them.

Diane revved up to eighty on I-80 and I-55. "That's not even speeding. That's just keeping up with the traffic."

"You've gotta do that to be safe," George said with a smile at his wife's twenty-year-old excuse for speeding.

At midnight they pulled into the OSF parking lot. At the reception desk, they found Sam and Lisa were in the ICU.

"I'm sorry," said the night-shift receptionist. "Only family members are permitted in the ICU. And not now."

"You don't understand! Sam and Lisa are near death! We need to see them now!" Diane protested.

"Let me call the night nurse... Hello?... We have a family that wants to see Sam and Lisa. Oh, I'll tell them. Bye." Turning to them, the receptionist said, "Sam and Lisa have been moved from the ICU to the hospice."

"Does that mean they're better?" Diane asked.

"Uh, no, Diane. That means they're there to die," George answered.

"Oh, we've got to hurry then!" Diane urged.

The zombie couple rushed to the adjacent building that held the hospice care.

"Where are Sam and Lisa?" Diane asked the head nurse at the front desk.

"Ah. Are you family? Friends?"

"Friends, very close friends."

"Go to room A. I believe Sam's father is with them."

They entered the room in a rush. Two older men sat in between two white-bandaged figures on adjacent beds. Their faces were obscured, except for noses poking through the bandages. Both noses were black and blistered.

One of the men had his arm around the other, who was quietly crying and wiping his eyes.

"Hello? Excuse us. We're Diane and George. We're close friends of Sam and Lisa."

The crying man looked up and said bleakly, "You were friends with Sam and Lisa. They just died."

"Oh no!" Diane wailed and rushed to his side. "She was my best friend."

"He was my son, and she was my daughter-in-law."

George wondered, *Who will run the Midley Beacon?*

"Is there anything I can do?" said the other man. He was an older man with white stubble covering his round head. Short, stocky, and amiable, his friendly face shone with openness. "I'm Elmo Gridley, a grief counselor for the hospice."

"He's been a big help," Mr. Melvin said.

"Thank you," Diane said. "Maybe this will help." She held up the ampoule of zombie blood. "Mr. Melvin, I'm going to shoot Diane with the zombie blood."

"I don't think it can bring her back from the dead," he said doubtfully.

"It works for turkeys," she said.

"And for people," George said. "I'm sure we all died in the attack on the SPEwZ headquarters."

"It can't hurt to try," Mr. Melvin said.

Diane injected Lisa and then took another ampoule and injected Sam. Even she was somewhat grossed out by the charred skin flaking off as she injected them.

"How long until we know?"

"I don't know about people. Zombie turkeys came back from being chopped up within a half an hour."

"Turkeys weigh twenty pounds. Lisa weighs about a hundred thirty, so six times as long would be three hours," George said. "I base my estimate on how anesthesia affects people. Bigger people take longer and more of a dosage."

"Bacteria as anesthesia?" Elmo asked.

"Sure. The bacteria have to spread through the body."

While they waited somberly, Don and Maggie came in. They too had sped from Gary in record time.

After appraising the younger couple about Sam and Lisa's status, Maggie said, "Hmmm. I think your estimate is off, Dad. You're using a linear progression. Bacteria multiply exponentially. Using exponential curve for the bacteria, it will double in half an hour, forty pounds, then double again in another half hour, eighty pounds, and double a third time in the third half hour. Lisa should be up in an hour and a half, and Sam about the same."

"That's pretty soon now!" Diane said.

"I hope you're right," Mr. Melvin said. "It's a real gut punch to lose your son before you die."

"Is this a real hope?" Elmo asked.

"Yeah, I've seen my arm grow back in twenty minutes," Don said.

"And I've seen a zombie bull with its head and legs ripped off grow new ones in less than an hour," Diane said.

"Amazing!" Elmo exclaimed. "I've heard of zombie blood being used to treat diseases, but not death."

"I'm pretty sure both Don and I died under the SPEwZ wall when the plane crashed. I remember seeing it fall on us," Maggie said.

"I don't even remember that!" Don said.

"I just remember coming to work that day," George said. "The next thing I remember is struggling to breathe and crawling out of a mucky ash pit."

"You were out on the factory floor when the plane hit there," Diane said. "It was a blaze of fire when I went in there after you. The last thing I remember is dodging between pools of fire when the roof collapsed."

"Thanks for coming after me, honey," George said.

"I'd do it for any husband I loved with all my heart." Diane smiled.

"Based on your descriptions, I probably lost all my skin and then maybe my head when the roof collapsed. I was under a pile of girders."

"But, Dad, that collapse might have saved your life," Don said. "I think it saved all our lives from the fire. The roof was metal. It didn't burn, and it soaked up the heat."

"Could be."

"Oh my!" Maggie exclaimed.

"What?" Diane asked.

"Look at Lisa's arm!"

The black crusty skin where Diane injected the ampoule of zombie blood all flaked off like a burnt chicken—or turkey skin on a grill. New pink skin appeared underneath.

"That's not all," Maggie said, unwrapping Lisa's head. Blackened skin came off with the bandages. Lisa's face was smooth and unwrinkled. A brown quarter-inch fuzz covered her scalp. Best of all, her chest slowly moved up and down.

"Wonderful!" Mr. Melvin exclaimed.

"A miracle!" Elmo cried.

"Let's check Sam!" Diane said. Carefully, she unwrapped his face. Old, burnt skin peeled away like an orange, revealing pink cheeks speckled with brown stubble. He too had a cap of brown fuzz. His chest slowly moved as he breathed.

"Hooray!" Diane led the cheering, and they all joined in.

Afterward, they settled back down, awaiting the Melvins' awakening.

George said suddenly, "We're going to need a story to get them out of the hospital."

"Why? Why can't they just be released?" Diane asked.

"We've had to go incognito to lull the master hacker into complacency. So will Sam and Lisa."

"What do you mean?" Mr. Melvin asked.

"These attacks on the *Midley Beacon* and SPEwZ Inc. were planned by the master hacker, Mr. Melvin. We decided as a family to go incognito and let everyone think we were dead. Then we can attack the hacker," George said.

"So what does that mean for the hospital?" Elmo asked.

"The hospital has to think they are dead."

"You'll need a death certificate for that."

"I know just who'll get us a death certificate. Bill Prescott, my high school buddy. He's the coroner in Midley," Sam said.

"Sam!" Diane screamed.

"Sam?" Lisa mumbled.

"Lisa!" Diane screamed.

"Please stop screaming, Diane. I don't have the energy for it," Lisa said. "I'm starving. Maybe that's why."

"All we have here are some mints," Elmo said.

"I'll eat those!" She grabbed a handful and shoved them into her mouth.

"I'm starving too," Sam said. "Can we send out for pizza?"

"No, we should just all leave now. We'll stop at a fast-food place for you. Elmo, can we count on you keeping a secret?"

"That they're still alive? My word is my bond. I'll keep your secret."

"Good. We'll carry them out on this stretcher. Tell the hospital we took them to Midley, with Mr. Melvin, to be buried. Then we'll get the death certificate and have a funeral there. Mr. Melvin, is there a graveyard there?"

"There's a graveyard on my farm. Five generations of Melvins are buried there."

"Let's go then! Wrap back up, Lisa and Sam."

"Gimme my mints!" Lisa growled. She took another handful and crammed them into her mouth. "Here, Sam, you take some too." She stuffed a handful into his mouth.

"Mmmph," he said.

Don and George carried out Sam and Lisa as corpses to their cars.

* * *

"I didn't know they had died," the nurse said to Elmo.

"I saw them die. Mr. Abner Melvin approved the funeral home to move the bodies to Midley," Elmo said.

"That's the first time a funeral home came and took bodies without contacting me."

"The funeral parlor worked quickly to get the bodies out of Mr. Melvin's sight—he was so disconsolate."

"What happened to the four friends of the family?"

"They went with them to Midley."

* * *

In Midley, Sam and Lisa recuperated and got used to being zombies on Mr. Melvin's farm. They bought a pair of pine caskets and had a closed-casket funeral. All the surviving reporters from the *Midley Beacon* attended. Sam had left his money to his father in his will, in the event of his and Lisa's death. Thus, through his father, he could use all the cash he and Lisa had saved. This included the monthly rental payments that came from Lisa's rented home in Midley. This was where Lisa had lived before she married Sam.

With cash they bought computers and disposable cell phones. Don worked as their IT administrator, guiding them to only use public Wi-Fi and then hiding their identities and communications through anonymizing servers and VPN networks. They also encrypted all their emails with the longest possible passwords. Lisa used the password phrase, "Lisa Melvin is the first zombie Pulitzer Prize winner."

The other zombie survivors from SPEwZ came from Gary to Mr. Melvin's farm to maintain the cover-up. Although they could trust their families to keep the secret, the chances of being seen and recognized in their neighborhoods were very high. Pooling all their resources supported them.

Sam's and Lisa's phones had been destroyed in the *Midley Beacon* attack. Lisa, however, had memorized Colonel Figeroa's private phone number and called him.

"Colonel Figeroa?"

"Yes?"

"This is Lisa Melvin. Sam and I survived the attack, but we've faked our deaths to throw off the hacker who's been attacking us."

"Lisa! I'm so glad you and Sam survived! I would have come to your funeral, but I've been really busy decoding the cyborg animal signals and the command instruction set."

"I'm not offended you didn't come to our funeral. Our national security is more important. We need to meet with you and debrief in a secure location. Do you have one?"

"We do. The closest we have is the Peoria Public Library, Main Branch. Can you get there securely?"

"Sure. Sam bought a 'new' car—a 1964 Cadillac coupe."

"That'll be a little conspicuous."

"He registered it in his father's name. Sam got a good price for it. We also bought a used 2004 Taurus."

"Perfect! No one will notice it! I'll be there tomorrow when it opens at nine a.m. Meet me in the stairwell."

The next morning Lisa and Sam were the first ones in the library when it opened at nine.

"We'll be here ahead of him," Lisa said.

Much to their surprise, the colonel was waiting for them in the stairwell.

"How did you get here?" Lisa exclaimed.

"I'm part of the staff," he said with a smile. "Follow me."

He led them down to the second subbasement. He put his nose against a tile on the wall. "Scan," he said. A flash of red light illuminated his eyes. The wall pivoted from the ceiling inward, revealing another flight of stairs leading down.

"Hurry," he said. "We only have ten seconds."

Sam and Lisa scrambled after him.

The stairs ended in a blank red brick wall. A voice said, "Identify your guests, please, Colonel."

"Sam and Lisa Melvin."

"Please press your noses against the glowing brick."

One brick glowed neon red on the wall. They each, in turn, pressed their noses against the glowing brick and experienced a brief flash of red light.

Then the floor dropped swiftly and suddenly about twenty feet, like a high-speed elevator, with no warning.

"Woah!" They tumbled to the floor. The colonel knew to brace and stayed upright.

Immediately, two MPs came in and cuffed their arms behind them.

"What is this?" the colonel asked.

"Sorry, Colonel. General Walters's standing orders. Any imposters are to be immediately incarcerated."

"We're not imposters!" Lisa shouted.

"We have Sam and Lisa's death certificates on file."

"Those certificates were forged. We're zombies now. Look at our red eyes!"

"Sorry, we have our orders."

"You can check our fingerprints," Sam suggested.

"We will do that right now." They placed their palms on a scanning surface, while still cuffed.

"Hmmm. The prints say you're Sam and Lisa. Let me ask the general directly."

"General Walters?... This is Sergeant Slocum at receiving. We have a couple claiming to be Sam and Lisa Melvin, accompanied by Colonel Figeroa. They were dead and buried a couple of days ago, but their fingerprints all match... They are currently secured. Colonel Figeroa vouches for them...Yes, sir."

"The general says you can go free. The general says they are *your* responsibility, Colonel Figeroa," the sergeant said as he uncuffed the couple.

"Of course," the colonel replied. "I'm taking them to the debriefing room."

"Yes, sir."

The colonel led them to a modern, well-furnished conference room with an exceptionally thick door.

"Although the whole base is well shielded from surveillance under the library, this room has additional shielding and security. Also, all of your statements will be recorded for national security purposes."

"No problem," Sam said as he seated himself in a plush leather chair. Colonel Figeroa sat across from Sam and Lisa at the polished wooden conference table.

Sam and Lisa related their and the Newbys' experiences during the attacks by the master hacker.

"You guys have been through the wringer," the colonel said. "I like your plan to hide and maintain the illusion of your deaths. Now, what I'm about to tell you must stay in this room. Don't repeat in this base, in your sleep, or to the Newbys."

"But they need to be in on whatever this is! We're working together!" Lisa protested.

"Yes, I agree. But bring them here, tonight, at closing time of eight p.m. I will bring them up to speed."

"OK," Sam said. "Now what's so secret?"

"First the good news: we have decoded not only the radio signals but also the commands used by the master hacker. It is through these remote commands that the hacker or hackers control their cyborg animals.

"There are problems with their communication protocol: the decryption process is so complex that it introduces additional lag time in the cyborgs' reactions, as much as a tenth of a second. If there is any additional delay due to

111

distance or slow communication, the cyborgs would be slowed as much as a second."

"That would be a big problem in any battle," Sam said.

"Indeed. We conclude that the controlling hacker of the zombies must be local to the battle. We verified this when we investigated the cyborg controllers we captured in Scotland. We also discovered that the master hacker, the one they called 'the Boss,' was present in Scotland, supervising the battle, evacuation, and destruction of their base."

"That's great news! Did you find where the central base is?" Lisa said.

"Yes. Surprisingly, it's back in Manhattan, Kansas."

"I thought we cleaned that place out!" Sam exclaimed.

"Is it in another missile silo?" Lisa asked.

"No, but that's a good guess. It's in the same silo, only about fifty feet below, with no apparent connection. We traced the control signals to a wheat field and then discovered the antenna disguised as a windmill. We then followed signals from that to the Manhattan installation."

"So Manhattan is the final control center for the cyborgs?"

"Maybe. Certainly, all the signals end up there. Now I have to tell you some of the bad news."

"Give it to us straight," Lisa said.

"The controllers that were transmitting in Scotland were destroyed, along with the cyborg animals. We had to go back to Manhattan to find some animals. We found a few hawks and prairie dogs with the controllers. We did not interfere but just tracked them. They were apparently simply watching the Manhattan installation for intruders.

"Then we got the bright idea of checking Midley and Gary. We found a coyote and crows with controllers, again apparently for surveillance. In Gary, we found squirrels by the SPEwZ headquarters and two chipmunks at Diane and George's house."

"So basically, they knew our every move," Sam said.

"Yes. Combined with the virus we found in your network, I'd say the hackers knew everything that you or SPEwZ knew."

"So everything has been a trap," Lisa said with disgust.

"True. However, I think the Scotland raid was meant to kill you and the Newbys, and it failed—barely. The Manhattan raid, I believe, was to mislead us into thinking the hacker was dead. That almost worked too. He did not count on the zombie animals finding their control truck."

"Any other bad news?" Sam asked.

"Yes. We strongly suspect the hacker is on to us, even though the cyborg animals seem unaware."

"Why do you think that?" Lisa asked.

"First, it's only logical that he'd know he lost the secret of his control technology with the capture of the van in Manhattan. The logical thing to do would be to change encryption codes. But he hasn't. So we think he's leaving them there to mislead us."

"And second?" Lisa prompted.

"We've found other cyborg controllers where we can barely detect the signal, let alone decode. We're working on solving that puzzle now. That leads to the last bad news.

"One controller we've found is implanted in the neck skin of the head of the National Security Agency. She's my boss's boss."

"Ouch!" Sam winced.

"Indeed. We also found one in the new CFO of the *Midley Beacon*, Vasily Badenov."

"Double ouch!" Sam said.

"And in the CEO of the new zombie blood corporation, E-Z Cure's Mr. Masters."

"So what doesn't he control?" Lisa asked, exasperated.

"Quite a bit, but at the rate of several thousand zombie blood 'rage' controllers sold every day through E-Z Cure, the number of people he could control will reach millions."

"What can we do?" Sam asked.

"You and Lisa and the Newbys are on the right track. We are planning an attack with our own zombie operatives. This is totally black, secret, per General Walters's orders, even from the head of the NSA. The political repercussions are enormous, and the zombie NSA head can shut it down if she finds out."

"Isn't she the first black female heading the NSA?" Lisa asked.

"Junia Lyndhurst? No, she's the second. Condoleezza Rice was the first. She's the first zombie NSA head."

"Huh," Sam said. "How did she turn into a zombie?"

"She had incurable lymphoma and got the zombie blood treatment. President Trump appointed her because she was the best candidate and to show he doesn't discriminate against zombies."

"Have you detected any signals to her?" Lisa asked.

"Just a few. Not enough to pick up any pattern to crack the new command code."

"What do we do now?" Sam asked.

"Let's get George and Diane here quietly. I've got a plan for that, but I need your help."

* * *

A black van drove into Abner Melvin's drive that afternoon. A dazzling blonde stepped out with a large wrapped poster board and a cameraman.

"Can I help you?" Abner asked from his door.

"Indeed you can, Mr. Melvin!" the bombshell said, bouncing with enthusiasm. "I'm Darla Dahling from Zombie Publishers, and I've got a special announcement for Diane and George Newby!"

"Um, I think there's some mistake. There is no Diane and George Newby here."

"No, I'm sure I'm right. Sam and Lisa Melvin assured me they could be found here."

"Uh, Sam and Lisa died and were buried last week, ma'am."

"Now I know you're kidding me. I just talked to Sam and Lisa this morning! I even got their fingerprints! Now, Mr. Melvin, I understand your caution, with Sam and Lisa going incognito, but they met me before I left and said you might be suspicious. Sam said to tell you this is like the prank he pulled on his mother for April Fool Day when he was twelve, where he hid her shoes in the freezer. We have a prank for George and Diane."

"Only Sam would know that stupid prank. I guess I can trust you."

"And Lisa said if you didn't trust me, she'd beat you upside the head."

"That seals the deal. That's what Lisa would say. Come in. George and Diane are lying low."

"I know! We want this kept quiet just as much as you do."

Abner pressed the button on an intercom that Don had installed. "George, Diane, we have some messengers from Sam and Lisa in the living room."'

George and Diane came up the cellar steps from the bomb shelter below.

"Hi, I'm Diane Newby. I don't think we've met."

"Hi, I'm Darla Dahling from Zombie Publishers' Clearinghouse. No, we haven't met, Mrs. Newby, but Sam and Lisa put your name in for the special Zombie Sweepstakes by Zombie Publishers, and you've just won as an all-expense paid vacation with Sam and Lisa to the destination of your choice, and—" Here Darla paused dramatically and ripped the brown paper off the poster she carried. "One million dollars!"

"This special check to George and Diane Newby can only be cashed by you at our headquarters, with your co-winners, Sam and Lisa Melvin."

"I'm afraid we can't accept, Ms. Dahling."

"Why not, Mr. Newby?"

"We must remain incognito. This is a life-and-death situation we're in, although you seem to be aware of us."

"Yes, indeed. Lisa thought you might be suspicious, so she gave me your special code word."

"What code word?"

"Rosebud. I don't know what it means, but she said you and she discussed it."

"Yes we did, last night when she and Sam planned to meet Colonel Figeroa. That was our code for communicating if she couldn't come back. What do you think, Diane? Sam and Lisa seem to be behind this—or they are held captive."

"In either case, we should go to them."

"OK, let's go."

Once in the van, Darla said, "Now that we're in our secure, shielded van, I can tell you my true identity: Sergeant Jenny Sylvester, security specialist, US Army."

"I recognize your name, but you look completely different," George said.

"I thought your voice was familiar," Diane said.

"Let me take this off. It's hot anyway." Sergeant Sylvester pulled off the blond wig, revealing a trim military cut.

"Where are we going?"

"To the Peoria Main Library, where Sam and Lisa are."

* * *

My Undead Mother-In-Law Blog—February 13, 2018, by Ron Yardley

"Today is the second-year anniversary of the Valentine's Day dinner I 'enjoyed' with my undead mother-in-law, Diane Newby, and the rest of my in-laws. How I wish I could have dinner with the four of them again! I wouldn't even mind another battle between Diane and Don.

"But it's been over six months since their deaths at SPEwZ headquarters. EZ-Cure has begun rebuilding their facilities to supply their burgeoning worldwide business. The new building will be called the Newby Building in their memory. Mr. D. Masters participated in the groundbreaking ceremony today.

"For Karen and me, life goes on. Karen is seven months pregnant with our boy. We'll name him George, in memory of her father.

"Although I feel melancholy today, it is tinged with the sweetness of the hope of new life."

Chapter 9

Manhattan

Colonel Figeroa opened their final briefing in the secret meeting room below the Kansas National Guard Manhattan base before their counterattack on the master hacker. "The only way into the master hacker's underground fortress is through this abandoned well," Colonel Figeroa said, pointing to a spot on a map on their briefing room display. The map dissolved to an aerial view, and then it magnified to perhaps fifty feet above the ground. A dull-gray weathered square of wood covered the abandoned well.

"Or the only way you know. I can't imagine they'd only have one entrance," Lisa said from her usual seat at the head of the table. Lisa always took contrary positions, with pleasure. The colonel never complained.

"Or only one escape. Remember the Scottish fortress had the drainage through the tunnel as well as a secret subway access," Sam added.

"Yes, you're right." Colonel Figeroa smiled. "But practically speaking, we've only found one surface entrance. We had an oil prospecting team in the adjacent field using underground explosions to map the ground. We discovered the extent of the fortress but only found the one entrance."

"Hobson's choice," Lisa said. "We only have one alternative."

"Actually, we also considered a deep penetrating aerial strike. We have weaponry that can go through two hundred feet of rock and earth. But there is no guarantee we'd get the master hacker. We want him, alive or dead." He paused and then added, "You should know, if everything goes wrong, we'll have you abandon the attack and use that missile anyway."

"Of course." Diane grinned.

"Now, the attack plan is this: at 1900 we'll send Diane and George into the well. You'll take the zombie corgis. The cyborg hawks and prairie dogs will be asleep, but the cyborg coyotes will be out. We'll start broadcasting interference signals at 1855. You'll have five minutes to get from the oil camp to the well. That's about a mile." He showed their path on the aerial photo.

"And we already demonstrated we can run a mile in four minutes, by loafing," Diane said.

The army had tested them, first on a treadmill and then on similar terrain in Kansas. George, Diane, Sam, and Lisa turned in sub-four-minute miles just "jogging." They were completely unfatigued afterward. World-class zombie track athletes had already broken the three-minute mile and were closing in on two thirty.

"Zombie marines will follow you at 1910. As before, you'll be wired with audio and visual. Sam and Lisa will be embedded with the marines."

"I'll send the turkeys and the bulls patrolling the area," Diane said. "That worked well the last time we attacked here at Manhattan."

"Yes, they captured that communication van before it could be destroyed," the colonel said. "You will continue to be about ten minutes ahead of the zombie marines as you proceed through the facility. It's a hundred and fifty feet down the well. The last fifty feet will be in the water. This chamber here appears to be dry, but the entrance is at the bottom of the well. You will arrive there and blow the door, if necessary, by 1910. You'll be carrying shaped charges that can blow through a bank vault."

"Got it," George said, his first words in half an hour.

"Once through the entrance, the facility continues another one hundred feet down. There are at least five definite levels, possibly more. Our seismic sensors can only give us vague details about the interior.

"Remove resistance, but without losing your lives. Realize you have a force of a hundred zombie marines following you if you get stuck.

"Our overall goal is to flush the master hacker. He'll be controlling whatever cyborg defenses he has. When he goes, the cyborgs become ineffective. We saw that in Scotland.

"Clearing the whole facility may take up to 2200. We'll alert you if we detect him fleeing. You'll also wear these on your chest and back." Figeroa showed them a small round device, like a small cell phone.

"It broadcasts an interference signal that prevents communication and control with any cyborg animals." He smiled evilly. "It should come as a complete surprise."

"Good!" Diane said. "I want him to shit a brick."

"Diane," George reproved mildly. Diane never swore.

"Getting this guy is worth swearing, to me."

"That, and much more to me too," Lisa added.

"You'll each carry your weapons of choice: Sam has a machine pistol and bowie knife; Lisa, a flamethrower and bowie. Diane, your weighted billy club—"

"It reminds me of my rolling pin!" Diane interrupted cheerily.

"And stiletto."

"Like a turkey-carving knife!"

"George, you'll have your two kukri knives you got in Scotland from the gorilla you killed. Finally, in addition to your normal Kevlar and ceramic body armor, we've added a fireproof coating that will protect you for a minute of white phosphorus fire, such as the master hacker loves to use."

"Sounds like a great plan!" Sam said.

"No plan survives contact with the enemy," George intoned.

"So true. Our 'go to hell' plan is to reverse course and charge upward as fast as possible. All of you have already demonstrated you can climb twenty-five stories in five minutes. We'll give you ten minutes to disengage and get out, and then our deep penetration missile will hit."

"To the staging area, everyone! Party time in less than an hour."

* * *

In his Manhattan bunker, Vik Staskas sent a complex series of commands to the NSA head to direct her to give encryption information to one of his agents. Vik experimented with zombies and people under cyborg domination. Both were hard to control. People and zombies had stronger wills than any animal. He could take over conscious control completely if he wanted. That would blow his cover and show exactly where he had penetrated the government. He considered that his option of last resort. Or he could subtly influence people to make decisions that helped him, and only have very loose control. This was his standard approach with government officials.

Then he lost communication with the cyborg zombie.

And not just her; dozens, then hundreds of warning messages flooded his screen. He also got alarms from the hundreds of cyborg drivers he employed.

Quickly running diagnostics on his network, he realized an outside broadcast targeting his controllers blocked his communication. *The US military*, he concluded without a second thought. Double-checking, he realized they were saturating the cell phone networks as well as his secured direct-radio transmissions.

Time for plan B, he thought. He switched channels for his direct frequency and cell phone communications. That too was blocked.

Apparently, they realized the multiple frequency capabilities of my controllers and blocked all the frequencies. Time for plan C.

He released a group of zombie cyborgs he had in reserve. He directed his cyborg drivers to switch to their unique zombie frequency. When he experimented with these zombie cyborgs, he'd given them a different communication protocol and controllers. He avoided the radio frequencies and used the UHF television channels instead. The signals did not penetrate buildings as well and required more signal repeaters. He had them in abundance around his fortress.

As he'd suspected, a full attack on his fortress was underway. What surprised him was how far the lead group had penetrated. They had already blown the first door and were at the second level.

Let's blunt their attack. He activated the white phosphorus bombs in the room where the intruders lurked. Watching the video in the adjacent rooms, he saw the two figures quickly retreat, still smoking. One was large and one was small. George and Diane. He was sure.

No problem if they survived that room. He ignited the room they were in. Again he watched the adjacent rooms. Surprisingly, they advanced through the still-burning first room to the next. Quickly he fired that one. Again, they retreated, back to the original room. The temperature was over five hundred degrees, but they huddled in a corner.

Smart of them. They knew he had no other bombs in that room. They obviously had fireproof armor.

"Let's see if they're zombie gorilla proof." Vik occasionally talked to himself under stress but disliked doing it. It was so cliché. He was not a cliché. The Newbys had defeated two gorillas and a python in Scotland, so he sent in four zombie gorillas, operated by his best controllers. They were armed with twenty-five-millimeter machine guns with armor-piercing shells, coated in Mylar, designed to go through armored vests. Each gorilla also contained a high-explosive charge that should destroy everything in the room, should they be defeated. There was no such thing as too much firepower.

The room had dropped to three hundred degrees by the time the gorillas reached it, racing through the previously burnt room. Melee ensued. Vik had an extremely quick mind, but trying to follow the battle with four zombie gorillas and two zombies moving at superhuman speeds eluded him. The Newbys jumped and bounced off the walls and ceiling like lottery balls in an air-mix lotto machine—with excessive air pressure.

Quickly Vik realized the machine guns were useless—except as clubs. His operators smashed the Newbys, breaking arms and legs—when they could catch them. The Newbys were far faster and agiler than the gorillas. George's and Diane's knives and clubs left fatal wounds through the chinks in the gorillas' armor, which the Newby's expertly exploited.

Suddenly the action ceased by mutual consent. Two gorillas were down, with broken legs and knees. All six combatants were bleeding copiously and tried to stem the flood with direct pressure. George's head had been cracked, and both hands were broken. He leaned woozily against the wall, willing himself to heal as fast as possible. Diane had a left leg broken at right angles, and the arm on the other side twisted out of its socket. She wrenched it back in while Vik watched. Then she took a splinter from a shattered machine gun stock and straightened and bound her leg.

Vik was just about to call his controllers and prompt them to attack, when the four now healed gorillas leapt upon the Newbys. Unfortunately, they were not caught off guard. While huddled in the corner, George had taken two steel conference-table legs and bound a kukri to each using steel wire from his belt. When the gorillas attacked, the Newbys swung their short spears and nearly decapitated the first two gorillas. Blood fountained from their half-severed necks, while the Newbys rolled underneath the two remaining pouncing gorillas.

Using their momentum, the gorillas leapt to the wall, pushed off, and charged, huge arms reaching toward the Newbys. Back came the kukri spears. This time the gorilla operators were prepared and wrenched the spears from the Newbys. One gorilla completely impaled Diane on her own spear. Undaunted, she pulled the spear through herself, closing space with the gorilla. The gorilla dropped the spear and grabbed her with two hands, intending to tear her apart. Diane's hand gouged out the gorilla's eyes, blinding him and his operator. With her bare hands, Diane clawed through the gorilla's eyes, nose, and sinuses, into its brain. Grabbing handfuls of its brain, she evacuated its skull and pulled out the controller from the inside.

Things had not gone so well for George. He too lost his kukri when the gorilla grabbed it. Then defending himself from decapitation, he lost his arm. The gorilla seized the other arm and ripped it off. When George tried to kick the simian away, the gorilla tore George's leg off. He tried to get his remaining leg under him and hop away, when the huge ape smashed his head flat with a two-handed fist.

Diane, inflamed with rage, swung her kukri with all her strength at the back of the gorilla's neck. Before it hit, a rocket-propelled grenade hit the ape's chest and blew it to simian jelly, coating the walls and ceiling. Diane's and the ape's remaining limbs slammed into the concrete walls with bone-breaking force.

The zombie marine who'd shot the grenade from the door called into the oven-like room, "Are you OK, ma'am?"

"Aches and pains, but that's to be expected at my age. Thanks to the marines for the help!"

"I'm sorry about your husband, ma'am."

"Oh, he'll be all right in an hour or so, hungry as a bear. I hope you don't mind, but I'll have to beg off running point on this attack. I need some R and R."

"You've earned it, ma'am."

Sometimes Vik wished his audio and video weren't so good. This kind of camaraderie nauseated him. He tried to detonate his ape's self-destruction bombs—nothing. The controllers had been disconnected through decapitation.

Hmmm. He'd have to give them separate receivers in the future.

The marines advanced rapidly beyond the battle room into the next two rooms. He detonated the phosphorus bombs in each. The most advanced room lit up nicely, but the marines had already disabled one bomb using a shaped charge. That also blew a hole in the concrete-and-steel wall. They had a way out of his mined maze.

Assessing the tactical situation, Vik realized there were no more bombed rooms between the marines and the control room—except for the bomb in the control room itself. The ambush planned ahead of the marines, with the rocket-firing zombie chimps, had been bypassed.

Bitterly, he called the control room. "Evacuate now. Ten minutes." That meant ten minutes to detonation, as his people had been trained. There were actually only five minutes left until the marines reached the room, he estimated. Dozens of cyborg operators slid into tubes that dilated open beneath their chairs. Each tube led to a seat in the hyperloop he'd built to Kansas City. Thank God for Elon Musk's public-sourced design! Vik didn't believe in God, but he was still thankful for Elon's invention and public disclosure of plans.

The evacuation of his personnel would reveal the hyperloop route he'd hidden in an underground aquifer. The aquifer prevented sound penetration and detection by seismic techniques. However, the sound of the vacuum pumps and the hyperloop cars would be detected. The hundred and twenty miles to Kansas City would be covered in twenty minutes. He hoped his people would get there before the military could track them.

The hyperloop let out his people in a field outside the Amtrak train station. Each person had a forty-five-day Amtrak pass. They were each to go to several different cities and then to one of the ten pickup points. They'd then go to one of his backup control centers.

With the loss of Manhattan, he was now down to Fargo (another missile silo) and Seattle, where he owned a private island on Puget Sound. He'd have to build another one. He got nervous when he had less than three control centers.

But first, his own evacuation. His private office was not connected to the rest of the facility, except by hardwired connections through reinforced concrete. He already knew that wouldn't stop the zombie marines. He jumped into his private hyperloop. It exited into the bathroom of a gas station he owned in Kansas. This tube was shallower; just under the fields around Manhattan. Near the surface, it was too shallow to be detected by seismic sounds. It descended under State Route 114 by the gas station. It was only a couple-mile trip. If he launched simultaneously with the other hyperloop, he wasn't likely to be detected.

"C'mon, boys," he said to his cyborg chipmunks, Alvin and Theodore. He didn't need commands when they were in his presence; they were tame and hopped into his trench coat pockets.

Sitting in his hyperloop car in the back of his office, Vik watched the control panel until the other hyperloop launched. His employees were away. He set off the room explosives. Hopefully, he'd get some of those bastards. He pressed the Launch button. This was always a thrill. Zero to one twenty in four seconds, then deceleration.

The car slowed—at the wrong time. That was two seconds too soon! What was wrong? The control panel showed a tunnel breach ahead. The vacuum had been lost. He'd have to use the ejection seat.

Splat! Splat! Splattity splat-splat! Dozens of objects hit the car, rocking it and leaving red smears on his window. The coasting car suddenly stopped. Frigging zombie turkeys! Somehow they'd gotten into the tunnel, through the breach!

No problem. Bracing himself and holding his precious chipmunks in his lap, he pulled the eject lever.

Blam! The shaped charges outside the car blew off the top of the tunnel and the layer of dirt covering it.

Blam! The top of the car blew off.

Whoosh! Up he went, riding the rocket-powered seat. At the apex, a mile high, he heard another, softer *whoosh* as the inflatable wings and tail extended from the seat assembly. A tricycle landing gear extended from under his seat. A small electric motor powering a propeller began running behind his seat.

Simultaneously, back in the hyperloop car, his body double, who'd escaped with him, was drugged into unconsciousness. It was always good to leave his opponents something they expected to find.

Vik steered his ultralight aircraft toward Junction City, his alternate destination. He dared not go to the end of the hyperloop since it had been discovered.

Looking down, using his night-vision goggles, he saw the cause of the tunnel penetration: a herd of cows, probably those cursed zombie bulls that accompanied Diane, milled around the tunnel breach. The top of the tunnel was exposed, and a flock of turkeys mixed in with the bulls.

Worse, Humvees, Bradleys, and even an M-1 Abrams tank sped toward the tunnel breach. They'd spot him soon. Time for evacuation backup plan C.

Securing his chipmunks in the inner pockets of his coat, he then hooked the shoulder harness from the back of his seat across his shoulders and between his legs. Pulling open the armrest, he took out a controller with a joystick attached to an arm brace. Strapping it on his right arm, he squeezed the trigger.

The ultralight plane disintegrated around him. He fell rapidly, his trench coat billowing upward, like Marilyn Monroe's skirt. He should be hard to track this way, visually or on radar. He grinned smugly at selecting a black trench coat. Sometimes clichés were good. He was over a mile from the marines, but he saw tracers arcing toward where his plane had been.

He watched the altimeter on his wrist. At one thousand feet, he squeezed the trigger twice. The jetpack fired up. His descent slowed, then stopped, twenty feet from the ground. He flew swiftly just above the fields to Milford State Park. He was below any radar. He landed by his hidden cabin there. Shedding the jet pack, he wheeled his bicycle out of the cabin. Riding his bike the ten miles to Junction City Greyhound station, he boarded the first bus out of there.

It was best to be unpredictable.

* * *

As soon as George and Diane blew the first door, Colonel Figeroa sent the zombie marines into the well. They carried an air tank with multiple air lines with them to get them past the fifty feet of water at the bottom of the well.

Sam and Lisa followed them. The colonel showed his trust in them by allowing them to be embedded with the assault force. He also thought their video of the attack on the hacker hideout could be useful in flushing out other hackers.

Sam ran the video camera while Lisa narrated. The marines left lights behind them as they advanced.

"After that cold well water, we come up within this pool. Here is the door to the hackers' secret hideout, blown open by our intrepid zombie pathfinders, Diane and George Newby.

"Following their track, we see the hackers using a scorched-earth policy: each room has been blasted by incendiary explosives. It's a wonder Diane and George survived.

"What follows next is a scene of extreme violence. Viewers' discretion is advised. Do not show this to young children.

"This is the room where George and Diane courageously fought four cyborg gorillas. We'll have Diane Newby describe what happened."

"Thanks, Lisa." Looking at the camera, Diane said, "The four gorillas charged us, armed with large machine guns. George and I dove under their fire, stabbed them as we passed, and then jumped off that wall." Diane gestured around the blackened and bloody room as she talked.

Sam followed her gestures. Later, he'd edit the raw footage.

"Coming back, we stabbed them again, but they batted us with their machine guns. I hit that wall, and George hit that one. At this point, I lost track of George's fight. I had my hands full dodging two five-hundred-pound cyborg gorillas.

"I managed to cut one gorilla's neck, and I broke the other's knees. That cost me a broken arm and leg and a dislocated shoulder. George and I rested in the corner over there. The gorillas also rested as we all healed for a minute or so. George used the time to make two spears out of his kukri knives while I bound my wounds.

"They tried a sneak attack, but we were ready for them. George and I each cut off a gorilla's head while dodging the other gorilla. Coming back at us, they grabbed our spears and stabbed us with them. I tore out the controller from my attacker's head after being stabbed. George lost both his arms, his leg, and his head.

"I went ape when I saw George injured. I tried to kill the gorilla with a single blow from my spear, from behind, when the marines landed in the room. Thank God for our marines!" she said fervently.

"We'll get some interviews with the zombie marine force as well," Lisa said.

"Since then George and I have been healing up and eating MREs, Meals Ready to Eat, we bummed from the marines. They're nutritious, but not so delicious."

"Not as good as your pot roast, Diane," George put in.

"So you're up to speaking? Here's a fun fact about zombies: when we take a severe head injury, our heads and brains grow back faster than our memories do. George had to regrow his head and just now remembered how to talk."

"No. I didn't have anything to say for the last five minutes," George corrected.

"Do you have anything more to say before we leave you to some well-deserved rest, George Newby?" Lisa asked.

"Yes. Head injuries, like decapitation, lead to permanent memory loss. I don't remember anything after blowing the door into this underground fortress."

"Another amazing zombie fact! Thank you, George," Lisa said.

"Continuing onward, leaving the poor slaughtered gorillas behind, their free wills savagely squelched by the hackers, we see the next room has been blasted by fire, but the one after that has a huge hole blown in the wall, by marine explosives. They targeted the incendiary bomb and preemptively destroyed it. This led out of the trap-laden maze and into the main populated portion of the hackers' lair.

"We're getting closer to the front line of the marine position," Lisa said as she and Sam strode down a corridor. "I can tell by the heated air and the smell of explosives and fire."

Sam shot the video camera over Lisa's shoulder as she narrated.

Smoke streamed out along the ceiling from a room up ahead. Several marines gathered there.

"Hello, marines. Are you able to give us an interview?" Lisa greeted them.

"Sure. I'm Gunny Barnes. These are marines Teletovic and Wilson."

"What can you tell us about this smoke-filled room? I see the fire is still burning in there."

"We believe this was the control room from which the hackers controlled their cyborgs."

"I see they've thoroughly destroyed it. You didn't get a chance to detonate any bombs?"

"We got one from the door when she blew. Good thing we weren't in there. There were bombs on all four walls and the ceiling and floor. The partial blast from the room threw us into the concrete wall. We would have been goners had we been in there."

"Is it safe to go in there now?"

"It's been about ten minutes, and it's mostly out. We're stationed here to prevent any zombie animals coming out this way."

"Are there still zombie animals around here?"

"Quite a few chimps. Without operators, they're no more harmful than regular chimps—which is pretty dangerous. We've gotten all the ones we've found tranquilized, but there's no telling what other things might be hidden in this base."

"Do you think we could enter and record it, with you as our guards?"

"Sure. Let's go." The marines went ahead, scanning the room for other entrances.

"Be careful, ma'am. There are dozens of holes in the floor. They look like escape tunnels."

Sam filmed the blackened, battered room. He zoomed in closely on the escape tunnels.

"Here you have it, *Midley Beacon* viewers: you are the first to see the hackers' last redoubt, their last stand, before their cowardly retreat," Lisa said.

"Say," Sam said. "Could we explore down these holes? They look like slides."

"Let us go first," Gunny Barnes said. "Teletovic, Wilson, with me." Down the three marines went.

After a few minutes, the marines called up the slides, "You can come down now!"

Speaking into the camera Sam was holding, Lisa said, "*Midley Beacon* viewers, here we go, exploring the hacker escape route! Sam, follow me closely."

Sam snuggled behind Lisa, shooting the camera over her shoulder. Portable LED floodlights had been set in the control room, and light was coming up from below now. Lisa slid down the chute, with Sam hugging her like they were on a bobsled.

They dropped into a half tube, about six feet across, and looked around. The fire had not touched this room. The half tube was smooth, hard plastic, leading to a concrete wall about a hundred feet away, with a tunnel in it. Behind them, the tube went another hundred feet to the wall. Above them, dozens of chutes led along the half-pipe for its whole length.

After video streaming all of this, with Lisa's commentary, she concluded, "Now let's see what our marines have discovered by what is undoubtedly the escape tunnel for this center's personnel."

Walking up to them, Lisa said, "Hello, men. What have you found out?"

"This tunnel," Gunny Barnes said, "is really long. We've used our laser range finders in it and have not found a clear end. We're getting vague responses from twenty-five miles away."

"Whoa!" Sam said. "That's a good way to Kansas City!"

"Hmmm. You're right. This is headed east."

"I'll bet I know why you're getting vague reflections from twenty-five miles," Lisa said.

"Why?"

"That's about the distance to the horizon. The curvature of the earth would cause some reflection if the tunnel goes straight to Kansas City."

"Whatever vehicle or train that was here has gone."

"It looks like a small hyperloop," Lisa commented.

"That Elon Musk thing?" Gunny said. "I didn't think that was operational."

"The prototype worked this year. No reason these hackers couldn't have copied it."

"Let me tell Colonel Figeroa what we've found."

After explaining their discoveries on his headset radio, Gunny finished, "Yes, sir. Will do. Gunny out." Turning to Sam and Lisa, he said, "The Colonel has found another tunnel—actually, your pet zombies have. We have to stay here and guard this area. You can go investigate that tunnel. It's in the opposite direction, to the west, near the surface. There's a herd of zombie bulls and turkeys there. You can't miss it."

"We don't want to!" Lisa said.

"But how do we get back up?" Sam asked.

"Watch this." Gunny went to one of the chutes. They emptied about two feet above the half-pipe. Reaching up to the lip of the chute, he pulled down a sturdy U-shaped handle. It had a squeeze trigger on it.

"You pull this trigger, and the handle pulls you up to the surface. That was the first thing we discovered. If you let go, you slide back down. There are handles every three feet, and they haul you up like a conveyor belt. This must be how their people got into this control room every day."

"Let's try it!" Lisa said.

Up they went. Retracing their steps to the well entrance, they were pleased to see the marines had erected a coffer dam containing a small elevator. Hopping aboard, they reached the surface, then drove their SUV to the other side of the base.

They saw the herd of bulls and turkeys, as well as Humvees and Bradleys and an M-1 tank. George and Diane had recuperated enough to get there ahead of them.

"Hi, Lisa! Hi, Sam!" Diane called cheerfully as they exited their car. She and George were dressed in military coveralls. They looked well, if thin, and George with fresh pink skin and short hair on his head.

"You're looking a lot better!" Sam said.

"Yes, we had a hearty meal after we finished a dozen MREs. A few more meals, and we'll be back to normal. We're thinking of stopping for fast food on the way to Junction City."

"Why are you headed there?" Lisa asked.

"Our master hacker has led us on a merry chase. Over here is the hole the bulls knocked in the tunnel. The tunnel made an earthen ridge in the field. A zombie bull had put a foot through the tunnel and then thrashed about with its hooves and horns until the tunnel tore open. The turkeys got in and stopped the escape train. The hacker blew open the tunnel over here to escape, but the corgis got to him." She gestured to the skeletal remains in the small hyperloop car.

"So is that the end of the master hacker?"

Colonel Figeroa came up to them, smiling. "You'd think so. But no. This poor sod was a body double, sacrificed to throw us off. Notice the burn marks here on the car. These mounts are similar to an ejection seat in a jet aircraft."

"So you think he ejected out somewhere?" Sam asked.

"We know it. The Humvees, Bradleys, and M-1 drivers all have night vision. They saw the ejection and started shooting as what they thought was the parachute. It actually was an ultralight airplane, which they destroyed."

"So that's the end of the master hacker!" Sam said.

"You'd think so. But no. The pieces of the plane we found were not hit by our fire but self-destructed. He escaped another way."

"How do you know he went to Junction City?" Lisa asked.

"That's the closest city. And we have him under surveillance. "

"You don't need us at all!" Lisa exclaimed.

"Not this time. But to mislead him, we'd like your story to end here. Let him think he's gotten away. We've been tracking him through our secret agents." Colonel Figeroa smiled again.

Sam didn't think he'd ever seen such an evil expression on the man's face.

"You've had agents on the inside of their facility?" Lisa asked.

"Yes, but don't let anyone know that. All your stories and video must pass our censors. And it's in your best interest and the Newbys to keep him in the dark."

"Will do," Sam said.

"What can you tell us about these agents?"

"They're actually double agents, and only I and two others know who they are. The master hacker doesn't have a clue, and we'd like to keep it that way. Once he's captured or killed and we're sure we've ended his crime empire, then you can write the story—when you are safe as well."

Having satisfied Sam and Lisa, the colonel directed them and the Newbys to the room in the National Guard base. The success of the operation pleased the colonel. He couldn't wait to plan the next stage. First, he needed to get the latest news from his secret agents.

"Lieutenant Liu?" He called his secret operative from his encrypted phone in the shielded room.

"Yes, sir?"

"What's the latest news from our double agents?"

"He's working his way through the Greyhound bus network, buying tickets with cash and hopping from bus to bus. Once he took a cab from one Greyhound station and then walked back. That was in Kansas City, Missouri."

"Where's he headed now?"

"New Orleans. He'll be there tomorrow about 2030."

"Excellent. Keep tracking him. How many shifts of operators do you have?"

"We're up to four shifts of two."

"Are any of them aware of whom they're tracking?"

"No, just that it is critically important and top secret."

"Excellent. Well done, Lieutenant Liu."

"Thank you, sir."

"Over and out."

"Over and out."

Next, the colonel called his superior, General Walters. "Hello, sir. Are you in a secure area?"

"One minute, Ramon." A minute later the general said, "All right, I'm secure now. What do you have?"

"Our hacker has successfully escaped and is heading for New Orleans."

"Still under surveillance?"

"Yes, sir. What can you tell me about the head of the NSA?"

"She was madder than a wet hen when she realized the master hacker installed a control unit on her."

"You had it removed?"

"She tore it out herself."

"Ouch."

"It healed in less than a minute. I've sent it to your forensic unit for analysis."

"Thank you, sir."

"The other government officials are being contacted now and being debugged."

"The hacker has a backup communications protocol we didn't know about, that he used to control the zombie animals defending the base. We are analyzing those controllers now."

"Excellent work, Colonel. If we finish this mission successfully, we'll both be in line for promotions."

"We will succeed, sir."

"I hope you're right."

* * *

Vik used the long, boring ride to New Orleans to catch up on his various anonymous accounts from his phone. He used his secure VPN on the bus's public Wi-Fi. It would hurt his reputation if the master hacker got hacked.

Vik kept tabs on his far-flung worldwide empire daily, but the minutia of decisions and electronic signoffs piled up in his in-basket until he had some time to take care of them. He cleared off these mundane emails and electronic approvals, all the while analyzing the loss of his base in Manhattan.

So he hadn't gotten rid of Diane and George—and probably not Don and Maggie either. But that wasn't the real cause of his defeat. The zombie marines could have done the point work that Diane and George did on the assault—and the marines were the cause of breaching his maze of traps. The root cause of this defeat was the US military had successfully penetrated his network and had hidden that fact until they could take it all down. In one fell swoop, he'd lost the whole United States. He'd lost control of SPEwZ and the *Midley Beacon*, but he still had resources. They still didn't know about his European or South American networks, or his superyacht, or his container ship, or his hidden shipyard and factory.

Continuing his postaction analysis, he asked himself, *Why had the military been able to penetrate his network?* Primarily, because they had captured both cyborg control units and the control van. He'd anticipated the control units being captured, but not the van. The truck relay station contained his encryption schemes in firmware. He'd had no self-destruct capability on that, other than the whole van.

133

Grimacing, he realized he'd been lazy. When he'd lost the van, he'd taken a *wait and see* approach. No sign of decryption had been seen in the Scottish attack or in the six months after he'd "killed" the Newbys. There was a tremendous amount of work in recoding and resetting his encryption algorithms throughout his network. He hadn't wanted to do it. He didn't do it, and now he paid the price.

His new zombie cyborg encryption obviously worked. They had captured the control units, but they couldn't figure his algorithm from that. If only he'd converted at least some of the key US officials to the new method!

No use crying over spilled milk—or lost zombie cyborgs. He began planning his new assault on the US, and especially the Newbys. No more Mr. Nice Guy.

He had just completed his US attack plan when his bus arrived in New Orleans. He took an Uber to the dock where his hydroplane awaited him.

Ah! he thought as he relaxed in his leather chair in his office overlooking the prow of the hydrofoil, christened *Budapest* in honor of the city of his birth. Actually, he was born in Belgrade, but he always liked to throw off anyone seeking to track him.

The powerful jet engine quickly lifted the boat off the water, getting up to cruising speed of one hundred miles per hour. He'd be at his yacht *Rule Britannia* in two hours. He'd bought the yacht and named it after he'd taken over the British crime empires.

He spent the two hours travel time reprogramming his scattered cyborg animals to his new zombie protocol. He'd have to design a backup protocol sometime in the future—the military might penetrate his new protocol.

For amusement, he let his chipmunks scamper around his desk and eat from a bowl of nuts and corn while he worked. Sometimes they'd pause to look at his computer screen as if fascinated by the flashing screen and network diagrams. He'd tamed the two chipmunks before he'd converted them to cyborg animals. They retained the tameness and followed his commands.

The *Rule Britannia* drew closer on the radar screen, and then he could see its beautiful white silhouette on the horizon. Home at last.

* * *

Two days after the second battle of Manhattan, Colonel Figeroa talked with Diane and George in the conference room at the secret secured facility below the Kansas National Guard base. "Are you guys up for another battle?"

"With the master hacker? For sure! I want to nail his butt," Diane said.

"If Diane goes, I go," George said simply. "We're completely recovered from our injuries."

"We've followed him to what we believe is his ultimate hideout: a superyacht in the Gulf of Mexico."

"How did you follow him without him detecting?" Diane asked.

"Drones?" George added.

"Can't say," the colonel said, and he grinned his evil smirk again, blue eyes crinkling. "Military secret."

"Hey, how about us?" Lisa said as she and Sam entered the room.

"Ah, I didn't know you and Sam were up, Lisa. Would you guys like to be embedded with the zombie marines again?"

"Sure, we blend right in now!" Lisa said, her red eyes gleaming.

"We'll attack tomorrow morning. I'll go over the battle plan with you four at 1700. Then we can have dinner together in the officers' mess."

At 1700 sharp, the Newbys and Melvins met with Colonel Figeroa in the briefing room.

"Hello, everybody," the colonel began. "We'll fly to the ship tomorrow morning, arriving for our attack at 0900. We'll ask them to surrender to keep the casualties down. There are an estimated one hundred women on the deck alone, and there are at least sixty to seventy crew members. The *Rule Britannia* is a five-hundred-foot superyacht, built in Britain for eccentric billionaire Sid Boffin." He paused. "We think that is a pseudonym, even though our research shows a valid birth certificate. Mr. Boffin made his billions promoting races and gambling. He's been accused of shady dealing with organized crime, but never indicted or convicted. So he might be our master hacker. Here's a photo." The display showed a saturnine individual with long dark hair.

"We haven't seen anyone like that," Diane commented.

"No, there aren't a lot of photographs of him. If this is the master hacker. We got this photo from surveillance video during the ship auction. He bought it used from another billionaire's estate and then had it remodeled in Italy.

"Here are the specs on *Rule Britannia*." He passed them each a diagram of the ship.

- Length 500 feet 152.4 meters, trimaran design.
- Displacement 14,000 tons.
- Propulsion: Diesel 16,500 kW (21,992 hp).
- Beam: 75 feet, 22.86 meters.
- Draft 16 feet, 4.87 meters.
- Speed: 27 knots max, 16 knots cruising.
- Crew: 70. Guests: 150.
- Decks 1 and 2: A helipad and a hangar for two helicopters.
- Deck 3: A saloon and 25 guest rooms with an Italian marble fireplace.
- Deck 4: A dining area, 25 guest rooms, and a ladies' dressing room.
- Deck 5: A movie theater and 25 staterooms.
- Deck 6: Main deck a shaded 6-feet-deep (1.8 m) swimming pool with a depth-adjustable floor, located aft on the main deck beneath a full overhang; [11] Gym forward of the swimming pool.
- Deck 7: This is an owner-exclusive deck, just below the main deck. Includes walk-in closet, study, outside bar with whirlpool, numerous skylights, and a private glass-bottom swimming pool overlooking the transom dock.
- Deck 8: Custom 46-feet (14 m) power and sailboats docked in the transom wet dock located at the stern, between the twin hulls, below the owner's deck.
- Deck 8: A 10-person submarine, located further inside the ship, ahead of the transom dock.
- Deck 9: Engine room and utilities, in each outside hull of the trimaran.

"Our attack plan involves securing the helicopter deck first. We'll land thirty zombie marines there rappelling from the first Osprey. As our team rappels down to the deck, we will broadcast for all aboard to put their arms up in surrender." He paused. "That's the best-case scenario. Fat chance, in my opinion. There's a reason we're arming our marines with automatic shotguns, with exploding shells and bayonets. We want them to be ready for zombie-type resistance at the gorilla level.

"Five minutes later, our Navy SEALs will assault and secure the wet dock located in the stern transom. From there, we'll advance to secure the interior submarine dock, preventing any escape.

"Simultaneously, thirty marines will rappel from the second Osprey to the passenger decks and thirty from the third aircraft to the main deck. That's when the zombie crew lands as well, from the fourth Osprey.

"Sam and Lisa will land on the helicopter deck, rappelling down atop two zombie bulls—"

"We've never done that before!" Lisa exclaimed.

"It's not hard," Diane said. "You just hang on with your superstrength. All these bulls have been trained to be submissive to human zombies."

"We're not used to superstrength," Sam said. "We're used to running and hiding and maybe blasting some guns at zombie turkeys."

"Or flamethrowers!" Lisa said.

"Not advisable on board a ship," the colonel said. "Use the bulls to overpower any resistance you encounter on the helicopter deck. The marines should have it cleared by the time you land."

"But no plan survives contact with the enemy," George intoned.

"So true," Colonel Figeroa agreed. "As I was saying, you'll descend atop the bulls in their quick-release animal harnesses, along with one hundred of the zombie corgies and two hundred of the turkeys.

"Plan on some resistance as you proceed downward. However, your main mission is to record the action from the Osprey and on the ship."

"Can I take my katana? Sam got it for me for Christmas!"

"Of course. Bladed weapons are more effective against zombies than projectiles. I expect zombie resistance: gorillas, chimps, snakes, and who knows what else."

"I've got my bowie knife," Sam said.

"You'll want a longer weapon: a cavalry sword or glaive, for example. Diane is taking a glaive and George a claymore."

"Glaive?" Sam looked up the word on the internet on his phone and found this picture of variations of the polearm:

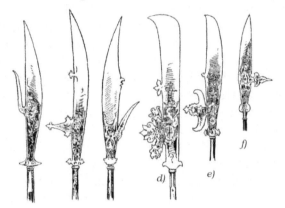

"Oh, that's cool! Could I use a halberd? I've always thought those were the greatest things since the internet."

"I'm sure we can get you one," the colonel said. "Diane, George, after Sam and Lisa are dropped off on the top deck, you'll be dropped with your bulls, corgis, and turkeys onto the main deck and seek out the master hacker. The yacht is very spacious, and even the bulls should be able to go through the interior halls.

"I have to say this: the worst-case scenario is the complete destruction of the whole ship, taking all aboard along with our aerial and sea forces." The colonel eyed them each in turn. "Are you sure you want to participate in this?"

"Where else can we get such a great story?" Lisa asked.

"If Lisa goes, I go," Sam said.

"I've already gone through death to get this guy. I'm not going to quit when we're so close," Diane said.

"If Diane goes, I go," George said. He winked at Sam.

"One question," Lisa said. "What's your plan for the worst-case scenario?"

"We'll rescue as many survivors as we can with our vessels. If we detect an escaping rocket or plane, we'll shoot it down. If we detect an escaping sub or boat, we'll sink it. And if we don't find our target, we're authorized to nuke the ship location. Let's see how he handles hard radiation and the shock wave from that."

"Wow. I guess if you do that, we're already dead," Sam said.

"Yes. We believe he will not want to destroy what he regards as his home, but we can't count on that."

"How do you know that?" Lisa asked. "Oh, I know—your secret surveillance."

"You got it in one," Colonel Figeroa said with a wicked grin. "If you live, maybe you'll find out what we used."

Chapter 10

Gulf of Mexico

Sam, Lisa, George, and Diane traveled by night on a military transport to the Naval Air Station–Joint Reserve Base in New Orleans. Arriving at 12:30 a.m., they met Commander Jaynes and members of the 195th Fighter Wing, the Strike Fighter Squadron 204, US Navy Reserve, and the Marine Corps Reserve light attack helicopter squadron 773. These units would accompany them in the attack.

Colonel Figeroa, who had ridden the transport with them, excused himself when they arrived. "Sorry, folks, but this non-zombie colonel has got to get some shut-eye before the big show tomorrow."

"I'm too keyed up to sleep," Diane said. "I have to get the zombie turkeys, corgis, and bulls settled down before they eat or gore someone."

"We've got to get our stories into the censors—yuck!" Lisa said.

"You're still going on about that?" the colonel said.

"I will as long as the first amendment is in the Constitution, Mr. Sworn-to-Protect-the-Constitution."

"Ouch!"

"We also have to get prepped on rappelling techniques," George said.

"Get about your business then! Good night."

The Marine Corps sent in four V-22 Ospreys that night. Three would carry the marine assault troops and one the zombies: George, Diane, Sam, Lisa, four zombie bulls for them to ride, two hundred zombie corgis, and four hundred zombie turkeys.

The zombie couples familiarized themselves with the rappelling lines and signals during the marine standard pre-rappel briefing.

Sergeant Ezekiel "Zeke" Johnson met them at the rappelling towers after midnight. The two zombie couples saw a square, muscular black man with a buzz cut and round face and head.

"So you're the civilians who are rappelling with us?"

"You bet, sir!" Diane said.

"No need for 'sir.' I'm only a sergeant. But I have to warn you: I'm going to treat you as fully trained marines, and if you fail, you won't go. Colonel Figeroa seemed sure you'd handle it, but I've seen marines fail this routine in training dozens of times. The colonel gave me full authority to flunk you if you flub up."

"No problem, Sergeant Johnson! We're not only civilians. We're zombies."

"Let's see what you can do then. First thing is, climb to the top of this rappelling tower."

"Here goes!" Diane charged the dangling rope, leapt up, and went hand over hand to the top of the forty-foot tower. In ten seconds.

"I meant, use the ladder—then come down!"

"Come down?" Diane called. "Here goes!" She jumped back to the rope and slid down.

"Not like that! You could hurt yourself! You're supposed to make a rappel seat and use your rappelling gloves!"

"Oh, gloves?" She looked at her hands and pulled the torn skin off. New skin had already grown underneath.

"Diane is a charge first, ask questions later kind of gal," Lisa said, smiling.

"I suppose you can do that too?"

"Let's try. I'll use my gloves, and I've got the rappel seat," she said, touching the knotted rope hanging over her shoulder.

Lisa too ran to the rope and climbed to the top in ten seconds. Then she tied the rappel seat to her hips, attached it to the rope, and slid down, using it and her gloves.

"That's pretty good. Let's see you do that, Diane."

"This rappel seat should be no problem, compared to macramé." Diane duplicated Lisa's proper form.

"OK, you guys next." Sergeant Johnson gestured to Sam and George. They ascended side by side on the two ropes, then descended by rappel seats.

"You guys and gals make my job easy. You're unconventional, but you get the job done. Let's review the rappel signals again and we're done."

Then they picked up the zombie animals from the truck and went to the cargo master in charge of loading the V-22s.

Diane and cargo master Sergeant Harry Fitzgerald tackled the tricky job of balancing a load of zombie animals in the V-22. Diane put the bulls into the four corners of the cargo bay, bound by their harnesses. She and the cargo master stored the corgis in panniers on each side of the bulls. Diane divided the mass of turkeys into four flocks, which they corralled with cargo netting into the four quadrants of the cargo hold.

"OK, that's the best I can do," Diane said to the marine cargo master working with her.

"It's the craziest cargo load I've ever seen," he admitted. "But it's balanced and doesn't exceed the V-22's capacity of twenty thousand pounds."

"We'll each ride a bull on the way to the ship."

"That's another level of crazy," he said in amazement. "They'll probably be shooting at you."

"That would be crazy," Diane replied. "Bullets are ineffective against zombies. They barely slow us, and they made us angry. Fléchettes would be more effective, and high-explosive missiles are the best of all, but the colonel said there are no visible weapons on the deck, and we will surprise them."

"Yeah, we'll sneak up on them, flying just above the water. They should have no more than five minutes warning."

The sun crept over the horizon as the four vertical takeoff planes and two F-18s and two F-15s took off. The four AH-64 attack helicopters that were to provide close air cover had left fifteen minutes earlier due to their slower speed.

The twenty minutes to their target zoomed by for Lisa. The cargo hold reverberated with the roar of the V-22 turboprops, preventing any conversation with Sam, who sat astride the bull across from her. Adding to the cacophony, the bulls bawled, the corgis yipped, and the turkeys "gobble, gobbled." Even knowing Diane had them under her control and she was now a zombie and could handle them herself, hearing the "gobble, gobble" gave Lisa the creeps. Lisa had too many bad memories associated with the zombie turkeys. Worse, the plane stank like a frigging flying barn!

A change in the pitch of the engines warned her they were near their target. No gunfire. That was good. She felt, rather than saw, the plane slow and hover over the superyacht. Now five more minutes.

The cargo door opened, and the roar of the turboprops went up like someone turned the volume up to max. The zombie turkeys fluttered out en masse first, while Sam and the bull—he had named it John—along with their panniers of corgis were lowered by winch to the helipad. Lisa had caught his eye and mouthed, *Good luck, love!*

Now it was her turn. Down came the cargo nets. Out went a hundred zombie turkeys, slowly fluttering to the helipad like red-eyed Thanksgiving decorations. The marine cargo master Sergeant Harry attached the harness to the winch and lifted her bull. When his feet were off the deck, he roared.

"Bull-oney," Lisa commented. "That's a good name for you."

Lisa and Bull-oney swung out on the winch over the hundred-foot drop to the helipad. There was some kind of fight going on down there, but Lisa heard no gunfire. *That doesn't look subdued to me*, she thought. She patted the katana on her back.

With a lurch, they descended rapidly. The corgis wriggled and barked incessantly as they heard their fellows yipping on the helipad. They began gnawing the cargo netting holding them in the panniers. The awkward ensemble landed. Quickly,

Lisa grabbed the harness release and freed herself and the bull, opened the panniers, and dropped them to the deck.

Then Lisa saw she'd landed into chaos. Bull-oney snorted and charged into the fight.

* * *

Marine lieutenant Francis "Frank" Zimmerman rappelled rapidly down to the waiting superyacht with his thirty men. His friend Lieutenant Philip Gerber led the second squad from the other V-22. The other squad landed on the main deck.

Frank always got hyped up before an operation, but this one was the strangest he'd ever been on. He'd done his time in Afghanistan and Iraq—that was where he'd lost his leg to an IED. When the marine doctors offered him a chance to get it back through zombie blood, he'd leapt upon it like a duck on a bug. Now he was landing a whole platoon of marines on a superyacht of a criminal, to prepare the landing of more zombies.

Things got stranger. Looking at the helipad as he descended, he saw a crowd of hula-skirt-clad girls—good looking ones too! The crowd resolved itself into a formation: a smiley face! As he landed and brought his weapon to ready, he saw each girl carried a basket of leis.

"Welcome! Welcome!" they chorused in their soprano voices. They ran up to put the leis over his head. He kept them away with the bayonet on his automatic shotgun. Laughing, the nearest ones tossed leis over his gun and over his head. "Aloha Oe" blared in the background on the outdoor speakers as the attractive ladies began to sway in a hula dance en masse.

Yellow flowers decorated his head and his rifle. He felt awkward and a right fool. Already the battle plan was out the window.

"Ladies! Please gather over here!" He followed the contingency plan for if they surrendered.

Giggling, the hundred or so beauties compliantly assembled in the landing circle under the V-22, their hair and grass skirts blowing wildly in the hot rotor wash. After tearing his eyes from their shapely legs, he saw his friend Lieutenant Gerber walk up to him, festooned in leis.

"Not bad duty, eh?"

"Something about this smells."

"Well, here come the zombie bulls. And turkeys."

Covered in leis, with guns pointing toward the giggling, whispering girls, the zombie marines watched the first bull descend onto the helipad, surrounded by a flock of gobbling red-eyed turkeys. Sam Melvin, wearing sunglasses to protect his eyes, sat atop the huge, snorting zombie bull.

After releasing his panniers of corgis, he said, "Hi, men. Looks pretty peaceful. Woo-ooh!" he whistled. "Looks just plain pretty. Hi, girls!" Sam called. They giggled and tittered in response. "Those are neat sunglasses you're wearing. Mirrored, just like mine and the marines'. Hmmm."

"Giddyup!" Sam prodded the bull toward the group of beauties. "Do you mind if I ask them a few questions?" he called to Lieutenant Zimmerman.

"Go ahead. I think we've got this deck secured."

The first assault group had already split up. Half was on the deck watching the girls. The rest had gone to the lower decks.

"Hi, I'm Sam Melvin of the *Midley Beacon*. What's your name?" he said from the back of the bull to the first girl he met.

"Li Sung," she said. "Sorry. We have no more leis to give you. We threw them on the deck to make the marines welcome. You can pick one up!"

"That's OK. Those are sharp sunglasses. Could I look at them for a moment?"

"Uh, sure." She took them off hesitantly and handed them up to Sam.

Sam rested his halberd in its holder while he looked at the glasses. Li Sung squinted in the bright sunlight. Sam couldn't be sure. He took off his sunglasses, squinting like her, and bending over, looked into her eyes. They were bright red, just like his.

"They're zombies! They're *all* zombies!" he cried.

The leis exploded, decapitating a dozen marines. Only two were left alive on the helipad. Lieutenants Zimmerman and Gerber didn't make it. Sam heard explosions reverberating from below the helipad.

"Mayday!" Sam called into his communication headset. "The leis have exploded! The marines are decimated and decapitated!"

A score of the female zombies attacked Sam on the bull. Instinctively, the bull swung its mighty head around, scattering and breaking the attacking supermodels like fine china.

Whirling and leaping like a dervish on amphetamines, the bull managed to avoid the hula girls' attacks with stilettos, garrotes, and bolos. Sam, however, quickly lost his halberd. Even with his zombie strength, he had to hold on to the bull's harness with both hands to keep his balance on the leaping, pivoting bull. His last view of the halberd was seeing it go overboard with a hula warrior when the bull kicked her.

The hula-clad defense force tried to throw the marines' bodies overboard before their heads regenerated, but the zombie corgis attacked like pit bulls in a meat market. The corgis worked as a pack and reduced several zombie women to skeletons. However, others took off their bikini tops and used them as bolos to catch the corgis. The bikini bras were strung with steel wire and strategically weighted. Attractive seashell and coconut-shell coverings hid the lead weights. The female bodyguards decapitated and dismembered the zombie corgis by using them like garrotes.

Then a hundred zombie turkeys attacked le femme fatales and pecked out eyes and carotid arteries. Sam just hung on to the bull while it careened around the helipad, stomping and goring the gorgeous enemies. Weaponless, out of control, never had Sam felt more useless.

Then Lisa and her bull and corgis and turkeys landed, and things got *really* hairy.

* * *

AH-OOGA! The approaching aircraft alarm sounded. Jumping out of his glass-bottom swimming pool, where Vik Staskas swam and watched the transom dock through his one-way mirrored pool bottom, he ran to the nearest computer. He quickly glanced at the pop-up window on his wall monitor with its live radar image of the air space around the ship.

"Crap on a stick!" he growled. *How* had the military tracked him to his ship? And it was US military: the glowing, real-time radar screen identified four V-22 Ospreys, four UH-64 Apaches, and two F-18s. They would be here in four minutes

Briefly, he considered launching his antiaircraft missiles. He could get all the Ospreys and the Apaches, but probably not the F-18s. They would certainly sink his ship—and him!—before he could get away.

Onto Plan Aloha, he thought ruthlessly. "Attention, everyone!" he broadcast ship-wide to all his crew, zombie and otherwise. "We'll have visitors soon. Use Plan Aloha." He watched on closed circuit TV as his bikini-clad zombie bodyguards scrambled to the helipad, leis in hand, quickly donning hula skirts and their special seashell and coconut-shell bikini tops. Kept in the ship's coolers for just this situation, each lovely lei had plumeria, tuberose, carnation, and orchid blossoms woven through a band of C-4 explosive. "Let's see how tough those Leathernecks really are," he said viciously. He was so upset he was talking to himself, just like a cinema villain!

Under Plan Aloha all the zombies attacked the ship boarders while the non-zombies prepared the antiaircraft missiles for launching at his command. It also required his crew to fight to the death to protect him.

He was proud of his zombie bodyguards. Each had been selected for her personal loyalty to him and her prowess in martial arts. They all volunteered to become zombies. They sparred daily in the gym on the main deck when they weren't providing protective camouflage by sunbathing on deck. They hid knives in their grass skirts, and combination garrotes and bolos in their bikini tops, and throwing stars in their hair.

Had his disguise of a sybaritic billionaire failed? No, more likely he had been traced from New Orleans. Maybe even from Manhattan! How could they have done that?

As he dashed to his office control room, his mind raced through the possibilities. He only had what he carried from his ship to Manhattan and back. He was bug-free—he was sure. That left external surveillance. Perhaps a drone? That was it! A small drone would not be detected by radar or sight and could follow him from the time he flew his backpack to his bicycle and then from the bus. It would have to be more capable than any drone he'd ever heard of—but it was possible.

More likely it was a group of drones deployed around Manhattan for the possibility of his flight. Hmmm, maybe he could train guard eagles to destroy drones in the future?

Watching the monitors, he saw his bodyguards neutralize the marines and corgis, but the zombie bulls and turkeys were eluding them. Two battles churned, one on the helipad and one on the main deck, just above his private deck. They'd have trouble penetrating his private deck, even with high explosives. He'd lined it with steel and composite armor above, below, and around. The deck contained only one access point, from his secret submarine dock directly below his desk. He prepared to take that route.

"Hop aboard, guys," he called to his chipmunks. Alvin and Theodore jumped in the armored waterproof cage he'd designed for them.

No sense in delaying his escape. A portal dilated below his seat, while a telescoping brass pole descended from the ceiling into it. From his childhood in Belgrade, he had always loved firefighters. Building a fire-pole escape fulfilled one of his many dreams. He slid down to his hidden submarine.

* * *

As George and Diane Newby landed with their bulls and corgis and turkeys on the main deck with the last two squads of marines, they heard a tremendous BOOM! It sounded exactly like a Fourth of July finale. Then fifty bikini and hula-skirt-clad zombies met them, not with leis but with katanas and naginatas, Japanese swords and spears.

The marines stayed low and close to the ship's railing, encircling the stern of the main deck. This way they created a vee of enfilading fire on the mass of zombies in the middle of the deck. Unfortunately, the zombie ninja fighters were so quick and nimble, most of the shots missed them as they charged the zombie marines. Closing quickly enabled them to chop up some marines. In response, the marines skewered them with their bayonets and blew them to kingdom come from point-blank range.

George and Diane, their bulls, corgis, and the remaining two hundred turkeys settled next to a swimming pool, partially shaded by the upper decks. While the marines occupied most of the zombie chicks by shooting at them with their automatic shotguns, Diane and George attacked the closest group poised to strike, providing some cover for the embattled marines.

"Charge!" Diane yelled as she and George bull rushed the nearest group of red-eyed bodyguards waiting near the pool. At the last instant, they rolled out of the way of the charging bulls and swung their weapons at the bulls' legs. The zombie warriors lopped off eight legs in less than a second. George and Diane leapt from the screaming bulls, skidding on their own blood, bounced off the bulkhead leading into the ship, and charged back at the now bloody beauties.

Meanwhile, one of the bleeding bulls slowly skidded into the swimming pool. There it floated, coloring the water red while its legs regrew. The other slammed into the bulkhead supporting the upper decks, splintering exotic hardwoods and denting the sheet metal beneath. It rolled around the deck like a giant, bloody snake, spearing any zombies who came near with its horns.

George hacked at a katana-wielding woman, who barely came to his chest, with his four-foot claymore. She neatly deflected the blow, and her counter slash cut through his body armor to his ribs.

"Crap." He sighed as he spun away from another katana slice, spraying blood and barely deflecting the blow. These gals were *much* worse than the zombie gorillas. They were faster than he was!

Enraged that her husband had been injured, Diane beheaded the female zombie from behind with her glaive. Two other bodyguards, in turn, attacked her from behind. George jumped between them and her, catching both katana blades on his claymore. The force of the double blow deflected him into Diane, who tumbled backward over him and rolled into the two attackers, knocking them over.

Screaming in rage and grabbing and lifting each girl by her steel-wired bikini top, she jumped to the railing and hurled them into the sea, off the stern of the yacht. Then a naginata hit her in the back and came out her sternum, pitching her into the brine.

George roared "Diane!" and raced to help her.

Four zombie bodyguards assaulted him, and he was hard pressed to stay alive himself, let alone help Diane.

Hitting the sea, Diane reached behind her and pulled out the naginata. It was just like unbuttoning dress buttons down her back, except her chest exploded with pain and clouds of her blood filled the water. *I'd better hold on to this*, she thought. She'd left her glaive on the deck when she'd grabbed her assailants.

She needed the naginata immediately. The blood in the water, from her and other zombie women, corgis, turkeys, and bulls attracted hundreds of sharks around the ship. One zoomed directly at her.

"Ah! Take that!" she shouted, filling her mouth with water as she plunged the eighteen-inch blade into the shark's mouth. It bit down on the wooden shaft, severing it, then slowly rolled away, bleeding copiously from its mouth.

I'd better get back into the boat, she thought urgently as she spat water, blood, and air from her mouth and swam quickly to the surface. *Good thing I swim like a fish—with zombie speed.*

Porpoising her whole body length out of the water, Diane gasped in pain. Her chest and back wounds still sucked air. The ship's wet dock was twenty feet away to her right, but ten feet ahead of her, closing fast, was the triangular fin of another, bigger shark. Diane had no weapon, her chest wound hindered breathing, and she was weak from the naginata blow.

She swam toward the shark, meeting it head on. That was the only way she knew to deal with trouble. It rolled over, exposing rows of teeth in a gaping mouth seeking to swallow her whole. Diane grabbed the lower jaw in one hand and the upper jaw in the other and tore off the lower jaw. Diane was startled; it was harder than she expected. Her fingers were cut to the bone on the razor-sharp teeth.

Bleeding like a slaughterhouse, the shark rolled upright and slowly swam away to be eaten by its fellows.

Painfully, Diane swam to the transom dock. She hadn't felt this bad since before she'd become a zombie. Her chest wound was barely closed. The bone and muscle had healed, but her skin gaped open red and ugly. She'd have a doozy of a scar. Her fingers still were cut to the bone and bleeding. She didn't know how effective she'd be battling these zombie girls. Hunger gnawed her gut as her zombie tissues transformed themselves to repair her wounds, cannibalizing her body tissues. *I should have taken a bite of that shark,* she thought ruefully.

She gasped for air as she hauled herself up on the transom dock, and she tasted gulf water. Salt water! Her zombie bacteria were dying! As soon as she stood up, two zombie ninjas charged her, one with a katana and one with a naginata. And she was weaponless. The lead one called to someone behind her, "Get her!" Glancing behind her, Diane saw the two woman bodyguards she'd thrown in the water were coming up behind her. They didn't have weapons, so she turned her back on the two killer women in front of her and charged the two behind her, slowly, painfully.

* * *

On the main deck, twenty feet above Diane's struggle, George battled the three remaining katana-wielding bikinied zombies. He had caught one off guard with a backstroke and decapitated her. He whirled his claymore like a helicopter rotor, but as it passed, each warrior would thrust in her katana, piercing him. The combatants looked like they wore red spandex outfits composed of their own blood, from George's blows. Then one bodyguard rolled under the flickering claymore and hamstrung his legs. George fell like a tree.

Each female swordsman thrust through his prone body with their swords, pinning George like a bug to the teak decking. George knew his complete dissection would soon follow. He painfully pushed himself up, impaling himself further on the three swords in his torso. At least they'd have trouble pulling the swords out of him.

Untroubled, the three blood-coated zombies each produced a ten-inch stiletto from her grass skirt. He'd pulled the sword points from the decking, but each stood a foot out from his chest as he got to his knees, surrounded. The three leapt upon him like three lionesses upon a water buffalo. George grabbed one with each hand and impaled them upon the swords sticking out of his chest. The one he couldn't reach, behind him, sliced his throat with the razor-like stiletto. Blackness clouded his mind.

* * *

Sam Melvin hurtled about the copter deck, clinging precariously to the Kevlar harness encircling the immense chest of the one-ton bull. Occasionally, one of the bikini-wearing zombie bodyguards would become impaled on the bull's long horns, but with a quick whirl, the bull threw her off the horn and into the water a hundred feet below. There the sharks waited. Several times, Sam teetered perilously near the edge of the deck while the bull fought red-eyed beauties, and no matter which direction he looked, he saw dozens of triangular fins circling the ship. The bull seemed surefooted near the edge, despite the gallons of blood covering it. It was a good thing too; the light railing was designed for people, not for bulls weighing thousands of pounds.

Sam hollered, "Whoa! Giddyup, John! Go there! Gee! Haw!" to no effect. The bull just ignored his commands, his drumming heels, his hands pounding its back. However, Lisa steered hers with seeming ease. Between the two of them, they kept the zombie hula girls from pitching the slowly regenerating marines into the foaming blood-colored sea. Most had grown back their heads, but they were still unconscious.

It was bad enough being burned and growing a new skin, Sam thought. *I can't imagine what it would be like to lose a head.*

The helipad, slippery with blood, took its share of victims from both sides as zombie bodyguards and corgis and turkeys slipped over the edge into the shark-laden gulf.

Outnumbered over twenty to one at the outset, the two surviving marines grimly fought back to back. They fired their automatic shotguns, methodically dispatching the bodyguards. One torso hit from an exploding shell splatted the garrote-wielding girl into hundreds of pieces. Unfortunately, even professionals like the marines found hitting dodging, twisting, high-speed zombies exceedingly difficult. More often, they would use their bayonets to impale the crazed hula girls as they charged them. Then with the bodyguards spitted like olives on a cocktail skewer, the marines would shoot them at point-blank range. The exploding shell would then clean their bayonets for the next thrust.

The women warriors showed their expertise with their bra bolos and garrotes, slicing off soldiers' hands and feet with a single motion. They threw razor-sharp stars at the marines' faces and drew long stilettos from their grass skirts, intending to cut off their attackers' heads.

The marines dodged the throwing stars and held and shot their weapons with one remaining hand while standing on their regenerating stumps.

The unpredictable zombie bulls, turkeys, and corgis tipped the balance in their favor. Most of the turkeys migrated down to the lower decks, but scores went from hula girl to hula girl, pecking each to shreds.

The zombie corgis were more organized and effective. Working together as a pack, they would quickly hamstring the bodyguards from behind, bringing them down and then gobbling them. Each one, taking two or three bites a second would eliminate a foe in a minute. They had learned to dodge the thrown bra bolos. Of the original pack of one hundred that came with Sam and Lisa, about fifty remained.

As one undead hula gal after another exploded into red mist or was eaten alive, the zombie women warriors realized they were slowly and permanently losing numbers. A single, tall hula dancer called, "To the lower deck!" and they raced belowdeck.

"Don't let them get away, Sam!" Lisa called. "Follow me!"

"How can I follow you when I can't do anything with this one-ton hamburger?" But then John followed Lisa and Bull-oney down the wide elegant and blood-splattered marble staircase. The bulls' hooves clattered on the smooth steps as they trotted down, dripping blood.

The deck below the helipad stored two helicopters and maintenance equipment, but it was otherwise empty. The noise of battle below echoed up the staircase.

"Next one down?" Sam suggested to Lisa's retreating back as her bull charged down the staircase.

The next deck revealed a luxurious salon with an Italian marble fireplace, matching the stairs. In the middle was an atrium lit by abundant windows with spectacular ocean views. From the railing, Sam could see down to the main deck, three decks below.

All around the atrium, the battle raged. A score of zombie marines fought hand to hand with knives against an equal number of hula-clad warriors with stilettos. The battle hung in balance when the rampaging bulls began impaling bodyguards with their long horns. The corgis hamstrung the barelegged opponents, and the turkeys pecked out eyes. Hundreds of turkeys flew and pattered about, attacking any zombie hula girl they found and gobbling. The feathers from the turkeys, alive and dead, floated in the air, obscuring everyone's vision.

Quickly losing half their number to the new assailants, again the hula leader called for a retreat. Down the spiral staircase lining the atrium they fled. Only two marines could pursue them at a time.

"Gangway!" Lisa shouted. She directed Bull-oney down the stairs, his huge chest brushing and bending the railings on either side. Seeing the bovine zombie hurtling at them, the remaining bodyguards dove into the pool forty feet below.

Sam's bull followed Lisa's, and half the remaining marines followed Sam down the two decks to the pool on the main deck. The other marines secured the third deck, checking each of the twenty-five staterooms. They discovered the non-zombie crew manning the hidden antiaircraft missiles and quickly subdued them.

Reaching the bottom of the formerly luxurious stairs, now covered in blood and dung, Sam and Lisa followed the zombie women into the adjoining gym. Flying naginatas rocketed at them. Sam and Lisa dove off the bulls, dodging the spears, but half a dozen pierced each bull.

The enraged bodyguards hurled themselves at the bulls and at Sam and Lisa. The hula girls' katanas quickly decapitated the bulls. Sam, weaponless, hid behind Lisa, who waved her katana briefly at her murderous opponents before they decapitated her. Sam had an instant of horror before they did the same to him.

* * *

Dazedly, Lieutenant Frank Zimmerman pushed to his knees and staggered to his feet. What happened? He hadn't felt this bad since he got that concussion in high school football. He saw a dozen other marines getting to their feet on the blood-slick helipad. Next to him sat his friend Lieutenant Phil Gerber holding his head and looking woozy.

Absently, he noted Phil's uniform and body armor were torn to shreds. Looking down, he saw his was too. "What happened?" he asked.

"Uh, I don't know. Lessee. We were assaulting this ship and then...blank."

"I remember rappelling down, seeing the hula girls—"

"The hula girls! That's it! Sam Melvin found out they were zombies, and then all went black."

"I'm don't even remember that. I just remember rappelling down."

"We've got to get on with our mission, Frank. Let's get our squads together and go belowdecks."

"That I can do." Together, they gathered the other dazed zombie marines and went in pursuit of the zombie girls.

* * *

Diane grabbed for the two dripping zombie girls as they advanced from the dock edge. They easily avoided her now feeble grasp and went behind her. Turning as quickly as she could, she was astonished to see them attack and decapitate their fellow zombie warriors with their stilettos and then pick up the discarded katanas.

Carrying their swords, they returned to her and knelt before her, holding out their swords.

"You defeated us fairly in battle," said the first.

"Even though you were outnumbered two to one," added the second.

"Then in the gulf, you killed two sharks, saving our lives."

"You are worthy to be our leader. We pledge our lives to you."

"What about your master hacker? Sid Boffin? How could you go from fighting for him to against him?" Diane asked suspiciously.

"We pledged to him because we liked him and he gave us things. We offered him our lives in service. He has been paid in full. We would have died without you. And you gave us your life and showed your superiority to us, more than he has."

Hmmm, Diane thought. *This was just like establishing dominance over the zombie animals, or over Donnie!* "OK, I accept your pledge of loyalty! Let me know your names. Mine is Diane Newby."

"I am Lulu Gutierrez," said a dark-haired beauty, the first one to speak.

"I am Sharon Windham," said a powerfully built Nordic blonde.

The noise of battle died down. Looking around the deck, Diane saw the Navy SEALs going door to door securing each room. Another group of SEALs was doing something to the ceiling.

"Let's go see what the SEALs are doing."

Seeing the three women, one SEAL said, "Did you take some prisoners? I wouldn't trust them if I were you, ma'am."

"They're pledged to serve me. They've already saved my life."

"OK, but stay away from this deck. We're going to blow a hole into the private deck above."

"Lulu, Sharon, let's go to the main deck and see how George is doing."

Diane barely had the strength go up the twenty feet of steps to the main deck. Concerned, Lulu and Sharon helped her up the steps.

Marines on the deck pivoted toward them, covering them with their shotguns.

"It's Diane!" Lieutenant Zimmerman said. "Do they have you hostage?"

"No, they've surrendered to me."

"You've one-upped us. We had to kill every one of these crazy girls. They fought to the death. You'll have to tell me how you did that later."

An explosion rocked the ship.

"There go the SEALs!"

"Where's George?"

"He's regenerating over there, with Sam and Lisa. All of them lost their heads before we wiped out the bodyguards. In fact, thanks to them, they distracted the zombies while we blew them to bits."

Despite her pain and weakness, Diane rushed to his side. "George! Can you hear me?" His red eyes opened.

"You found me again, Diane. You're hurt! Why aren't you regenerating? Your eyes are green, not red!"

"I took a swim, with a naginata through me. It cured me of my zombiism."

"Here's an ampoule of zombie blood." George took one from his neck.

"Don't leave home without it!" Diane said with a smile as she stuck it into her arm.

"Say, Lulu, Sharon, why are you still zombies? You were in the water too."

"Our former boss, Sid Boffin, foresaw this problem, with us in the middle of the gulf." Lulu reached into her grass skirt and pulled out an ampoule. "We each have ten ampoules in our skirts. We were required to swim daily in the gulf and reinject our own blood to rezombify."

"Clever," George said. "Where is your boss?"

"He stays on his own private deck, which he never leaves. He comes and goes without anyone knowing how."

"That's where the explosion came from! I saw the SEALs setting it up. Are you up to going to see the SEALs, George?"

George slowly stood. He bounced on the balls of his feet, testing himself. "Almost back to full strength. But I'm starving."

"Me too," Sam said.

"But let's get the story first," Lisa said. "My Bull-oney has regenerated. I can ride him down the stairs."

"You just like riding the bull," Sam said.

"You like shooting it!"

The two couples laughed, releasing the tension of battle death and dismemberment.

* * *

Vik Staskas landed with a thump in his secret submarine dock. The twenty-odd feet from his deck seemed to take forever when he was fleeing for his life. As he entered his private submersible, he cast back to the last time he'd fled for his life. Manhattan, of course, but they didn't really have a chance of catching him there. Before that, he'd have to go back to when he assassinated the leader of British organized crime, so Vik's flunky could assume the leadership position. He'd barely escaped some nasty traps, including poison gas, machine guns, and an incendiary explosive. Only his highly honed paranoia protected him.

Well. This wasn't that bad. Yet.

Vik gave the signal for the waiting missile operators to fire at the aircraft. With rockets launching and aircraft exploding as distractions, he opened the ship's hull and dropped his sub into the gulf. He blew all ballast tanks and dove quickly. Watching his sub's screens carefully, he saw only four missiles fire, instead of the ten he'd planned. Of those four, only two were hits, a V-22 and a UH-64 helicopter. That was no good. The missiles' batteries from the whole back two-thirds of the ship had apparently already been overcome.

Reluctantly, Vik detonated all his zombie bodyguards. He'd put powerful explosives in each one, only triggerable from his computer. He comforted himself over their deaths, knowing they had died for a good cause: his escape. He felt the reverberations clearly through the water. That should disguise his exit. He hadn't booby-trapped his yacht, thinking they'd never penetrate his billionaire cover. One more lesson learned.

From his submarine, Vik switched from one of his ship's cameras to another and watched as dozens of explosions geysered from the water. One blast rocked his submarine under the ship. Hmmm. Quite a few of those detonations were in the water. Many of his guards must have been thrown off the ship. Looking out the viewport, he saw swarms of sharks— and pieces of shark. Some of his bodyguards had been eaten by sharks. Had that shark been any closer to his sub, the explosion could have cracked the hull. Still, there were many explosions within his ship, destroying his foes.

His sub was electric powered, nearly silent, and with a sonar profile that looked like a great white shark. No wonder— he'd modeled the sub after that species. The military would come looking for him, so he dove as quickly as possible. One hundred, two hundred, three hundred, four hundred feet. That still gave him two hundred feet before he reached the depth limit of his sub. He trimmed his ballast tanks. The navy would not look this deep, and if they did, they'd detect a lone shark swimming at shark speeds.

He slowly sped up to ten knots. The lithium batteries drove nitinol "muscles" in the shark's tail, which propelled the sub forward. Twenty-five feet long, six feet in diameter, it mimicked a great white. Aside from test trips and recreational excursions, this was the only time he'd needed it. He'd named it *The Great White Hope*.

He checked on his passive network link to the ship. The sub's computer had the same network address and ID as his desktop computer. The backup for the ship's computer was his sub's computer. Vik left his onboard computer running, but he ejected the solid-state memory into the ocean and replaced it with a blank memory card. Any network analysis would show traffic to his sub as traffic to the shipboard computer.

Gritting his teeth, he brought up the video feed from his private deck and the rest of the ship. His beautiful ship was a mess, and his poor zombie bodyguards were splattered far and wide. Marines and SEALs had blown holes into his private deck. He saw Sam and Lisa, Diane and George. Curses! They'd foiled him again. Worse, two of his bodyguards had betrayed him and were apparently following Diane. They must have gotten into his shielded private deck before he sent his detonation signal.

Sighing, he let out his chipmunks from their protective cage. "At least you're safe and still on my side." He snorted. Talking to his chipmunks. That was like when he was a robotics student in Paris. Alvin wandered off. Probably looking for food. They had food and water in the cage but always looked for other snacks. Theodore stayed by Vik's keyboard, watching the screens for a while as if he understood. Then he too left.

Looking at his passive acoustic imaging screen, he "saw" an attack submarine twenty miles away, no doubt listening for an escaping sub. *Good luck with that,* he thought smugly. The ambient noise from the battle—and his superyacht—far exceeded the swimming sound of his shark ship.

He adjusted his navigation vector to his secret sub base in the Mississippi delta slightly to maintain a twenty-mile distance from the searching sub. They were always improving their acoustic detection technology and were well capable of hearing a "clang" from a dropped wrench, mouse, or keyboard within his sub. He'd thought of that and covered the interior with rubber, as well as the exterior.

Vik also programmed his autopilot to zigzag randomly on the course, so if they did detect him, they wouldn't suspect his shark was a sub.

It'd take five hours to reach his base, but he should make it without detection. Suddenly, without any action from him, the ballast tanks blew and the sub dove! Then the whole sub went black. No power. So. He was headed for the two-thousand-foot bottom, with no power. He wouldn't reach it, of course. The sub would implode somewhere between six hundred and one thousand feet.

He couldn't have that. Power first. Pulling out his flashlight, he crawled under his command console toward the main circuit breaker. It was still on. Flicking it on and off did nothing. Pulling off the circuit breaker panel, he saw Alvin busily chewing the power lines from the lithium batteries. As soon as the light hit him, the chipmunk scampered away.

"GAH!" Vik roared.

* * *

"How's it going?" Colonel Figeroa asked Chief Petty Officer Brian Watkins.

"Great! We just blew the ballast tanks and took away his power," the CPO told him proudly. "I'm running Theodore, the chipmunk that blew the ballast tanks."

The other cyborg operator, Second Lieutenant Alfredo Polano, said, "Can't talk now. I'm dodging around the sub."

"If we get him, I'll give you both commendations."

"He doesn't have much of a chance. He's down to five hundred feet and descending a hundred feet a minute," the CPO said.

"Five more minutes should tell. Remember, he's a real genius. He might have something up his sleeve," the colonel said.

Over the previous six months, Colonel Figeroa scoured the US Army, Air Force, Marine, Navy, and Coast Guard for the best video game players to man Sid Boffin's chipmunks. He found the CPO in the navy and the lieutenant in the army. The men practiced on two chipmunks the NSA captured and altered to match the control units on the rats, chimps, and gorillas. They did not commandeer Sid Boffin's chipmunks; they'd just been in passive observation mode up until now. They never learned Sid Boffin's real name. One thing they learned from the chipmunks' observations were their names, Alvin and Theodore. In keeping with Sid Boffin's whimsy, they named the practice chipmunks Simon and Dave. All that effort paid off.

* * *

Working faster than ever before to save his life, Vik spliced the severed wires together. He'd get the chipmunk later. Power first.

The lights came on. He leapt to the control panel and blew the ballast tanks. The sub stopped its descent and began to rise. Out of the corner of his eye, he saw movement. Like a viper, he drew his Beretta and shot Theodore. After passing through the chipmunk, the bullet ricocheted once off the steel behind the rubber and stopped.

His thoughts raced. The military had obviously commandeered his chipmunks and used them as spies. He hurt, surprisingly, from killing his second cyborg. *I can always get another chipmunk*, he thought, trying to soothe his pain.

They knew where he was. He put his gun on the desk, close at hand, in case Alvin showed up. He brought his sub surfaceward as quickly as possible. He'd have to abandon it and take his powered escape torpedo. It too was silent.

The depth meter showed six hundred, five hundred, then four hundred feet. At least he knew his overengineered design was good to at least seven hundred and forty-three feet. That was his maximum depth when he blew the tanks.

Light began filtering in through the front-view portal. He was nearing the surface.

* * *

"We may have to land the SEALs around him when he surfaces," the colonel said.

"Let me try one more thing," Lieutenant Polano said.

"What's that?"

"I can climb to the desk, and get to the gun, and pull the trigger..."

"And kill him?"

"Yeah. That's the idea. But I can't have him see me. There. He's looking away from the desk—AH!"

"What happened?"

"I pulled the trigger just as he grabbed me, and then lost contact."

* * *

Hearing a scampering on his desk, Vik grabbed his pistol without looking. And got a handful of chipmunk too. As he swept both the gun and the chipmunk up, the gun went off. Directly at the front-view portal. A stream of water, a thumb-width thick, with two hundred pounds of force behind it, nearly decapitated him.

Filled with rage, he crushed the chipmunk in his hand. Blood covered his hand and gun. Now what was he going to do?

He had already blown the ballast tanks. No more lift was available, and water filled the sub.

He jerked the yoke and *swam* upward at the top speed of the sub, twenty knots, heading toward the lighted surface, four hundred feet away. The water in the sub sloshed backward, toward the tail. Then the view portal spider-webbed with cracks. Diving beneath the console, he just avoided its collapse as tons of cold water filled the sub. The lights flickered and went out. His jury-rigged splice shorted. The sub sank like a lead zeppelin.

The cold shock of the water stunned Vik. The pressure at that depth was a man standing on each square inch of his body. It pushed the air out of his lungs in one big bubble, filling them with sea water. The cold sapped his energy. He didn't have the strength to choke. Vik began to lose consciousness. Only one thing left to do. He took an ampoule from around his neck and stabbed himself in the leg. Zombie blood flowed into him as he lost consciousness in the cold darkness.

* * *

"Captain Marinara! Track that sub with active sonar!" Colonel Figeroa commanded.

"We're working on it, sir," the captain said. "There's a lot of ambient noise from the yacht."

"You can't detect it even though you know exactly where it is?"

"That's correct, sir. We're moving closer. We have the last location noted from your remote transmissions. We should be there in twenty minutes."

"Very good. I'll send the helicopters over the area too." The colonel commanded the remaining UH-64 helicopter to go to the sub's last known location several miles away. They found nothing: no debris, no life boats, nothing.

The attack sub, the Virginia-class USS *North Dakota*, crisscrossed the area. They dove to the bottom, two thousand feet below. Nothing.

* * *

Sam and Lisa, the Newbys, and the two zombie bodyguards had just walked into the ship's control room on the private deck when dozens of explosions rocked the ship. The monitors displaying the ship's security cameras showed marines thrown about by exploding bodies of the zombie bodyguards.

Colonel Figeroa knew the hidden sub was about twenty-five feet long and silent. They had found its secret dock. They found no documentation on its capabilities or its appearance.

His intelligence service analyzed every frame of transmission from the chipmunk spies before their demise. The sub was covered with rubber coating and had no engine noise whatsoever.

There was one frame from Alvin showing the punctured front viewport before the transmission ceased. Analyzing it and the last depth reading, his specialists said there was a less than 50 percent chance Vik got to the surface, which was confirmed by the lack of debris. Their consensus opinion was the sub sank to the bottom two thousand feet below. It could easily be missed in the vast Gulf of Mexico. It could also have broken up.

Had they finally gotten Sid Boffin? Or had he faked his death yet again?

The USS *North Dakota* had other duties. Colonel Figeroa hired civilian treasure hunters with deep-water scanners to thoroughly scan the gulf bottom within five miles of the sub's last location. He told them he was looking for a Spanish treasure ship, but what he really wanted was a detailed photographic record of the gulf bottom.

He got his photographs. His underwater experts analyzed them, foot by foot. Nothing was ever found.

Chapter 11

Washington, DC

After six months away, Sam finally made it to the *Midley Beacon* office. As usual, Lisa had gotten in before him. Even as a zombie, she needed less sleep and usually got in by 6:00 a.m., before Sam even awoke.

The building's facade and interior had been repaired and refurbished since the gasoline truck explosion that killed Lisa and him, but the exterior sandstone and granite still bore chips and marks. The explosion killed eight of their reporters and staff. In all their injuries and zombification, hiding from Sid Boffin and then secret work for the NSA, they'd missed the funerals of some close friends. Sam quietly grieved for them as he entered the office.

Ron Yardley typed away on his *Midley Beacon* laptop.

"Hi, Ron," Sam called out.

"Hi, Sam. I'm busy getting my first official blog post out for the *Midley Beacon*."

"Great! Could I read it when you're done?"

"Sure! You're my boss, after all."

"Uh, yeah. I forgot. I'm not a natural boss."

"That's why I like you so much! You're unnatural! You're supernatural!"

"Please, don't remind me! I'm still shocked when I look in the mirror each morning and red eyes stare back, and I'm not hungover."

"Anyway, I just finished. It's on its way."

Stopping by Lisa's office, Sam poked his head in. "Good morning, honey!"

"Good morning, Sam!" Lisa smiled cheerily.

"You seem to be in a good mood!"

"You didn't yell in from the office! That's all it takes!"

"We've been married two years, almost, and I just found out now?"

"I've been yelling at you for two years. This is the first time you've listened!"

"Actually, you were yelling at me for years before we got married."

"Fifteen years, to be accurate."

"The years I've known you have been the best of my life."

"You mush ball! I can always count on you for mush!"

"Anything you need? I'm going to read Ron's blog post."

"Get on with it already! What are you doing wasting time in here?"

"It's never a waste, spending time with you."

"OK, you've spent time with me. Now get to work!"

"Of course. I love you!"

"I love you too, Sam."

"Hello, world!" Sam read from Ron's blog post. "This is Ron Yardley, blogger of 'My Undead Mother-In-law.' I've set up shop here at the *Midley Beacon* instead of my original WordPress home for the simple reason they're paying me a salary. And benefits.

"Why? Well, you may ask. It seems I have a certain cache by having an undead mother-in-law, Diane Newby, who's also the world's most famous zombie and now a national heroine. And my father-in-law, George, too. And Sam and Lisa Melvin of the *Midley Beacon,* my new boss and bossess.

"(You don't think 'bossess' is a word? Sure it is! I just invented it.)

"Anyway, I'm here to give you the news on my zombie family, just as I always have. So what's new? Mom and Dad are busy rebuilding SPEwZ. The insurance money has come in, and the SPEwZ block in Gary hums with construction workers rebuilding the facilities.

"My mother-in-law has finally been completely accepted by her church. They've put her in charge on a zombie outreach mission in Gary, Indiana. The church gives emotional and financial support to people finding the zombie experience disruptive and confusing.

"Interestingly, the two surviving zombie bodyguards of Sid Boffin, Lulu Guitierrez and Sharon Windham, continue their bodyguard work for my mother-in-law. Because of their highly developed paranoia, they maintain their guard even when she is working and volunteering at the church. Or when she's out dominating rogue zombie animals.

"My father-in-law plans SPEwZ's business strategy, manages the money, and pays the bills for SPEwZ. His son, Don, my zombie brother-in-law, plans the corporation's technical infrastructure. Maggie Newby, Don's wife, ensures the medical aspects of collecting and dispersing zombie blood meet federal medical regulations.

"The former zombie blood market leader, E-Z Cure, collapsed with the arrest of CEO D. Master, a.k.a. 'Master of Disaster,' nee Antonio Pucci. It turns out Mr. Pucci, who formerly acted in Italian Westerns, was hired by Sid Boffin to be his front man to his crime empire. Now E-Z Cure's zombie blood customers and suppliers are flocking back to SPEwZ Inc.

"My employer, the *Midley Beacon*, bid adieu to its former CFO Vasily Badenov as well. Like Mr. Pucci, Mr. Badenov had a cyborg controller installed in his body and was completely controlled by Sid Boffin. The FBI used communication to and from the controllers to trace all one thousand eight hundred and forty-seven of Sid Boffin's moles. (Follow this link to the FBI web page documentation.) The FBI elicited Badenov's and Pucci's complete cooperation in researching and dismantling Sid Boffin's worldwide crime empire, in exchange for a criminal plea bargain.

"Working closely with Scotland Yard, the NSA helped the UK unravel the UK and EU branches of the Boffin crime syndicate. The tentacles of corruption spread further than anyone dreamt, into every country in Europe and the Middle East.

"The NSA agency also discovered Sid Boffin's hidden base for his container ship he used to pirate the *Stella Moru*, on a small island off the coast of Baja, California. They found *Stella Moru*'s captain, Dimitri Koumondoros, there, being held captive by a capuchin monkey and a black mamba. The US Coast Guard and Navy captured the base without incident or injury by broadcasting interfering signals to the cyborg controllers. They arrested the team of cyborg controllers Sid had used for the hijackings and charged them with murder and piracy.

"There is a human-interest aspect of this story: Captain Koumondoros's life was spared because he played high-level competitive checkers. One of the cyborg controllers loved checkers. This fact, combined with the controllers' cooperation with the NSA, is mitigating their punishment.

"Finally, me and Karen [which Sam changed to the grammatically correct "Karen and I"] have moved from Toledo to Midley, Illinois! I thought western Ohio was flat, but central Illinois is flatter, with fewer trees. But the weather is warmer and sunnier, and the people are friendly. The 'big' city of Peoria is only a half an hour away, if we want some exciting nightlife. I walk three blocks to work each day and walk home for lunch. And they pay me more than I was getting through my own internet marketing firm.

"That's a ton of news and a longer blog post than I usually write. Keep the emails and comments flowing here to the *Midley Beacon* site, just as you have in the past. Ron Yardley."

"Hey, Ron!" Sam called.

"Whatcha got?"

"I like it, except for 'Hello, world!' That seems like a dumb way to open."

"It's classic internet jargon! It's the way I always start! It's my brand!"

"I was there at the start of the internet, and I don't remember it! Try something else."

"OK. How about, 'Greetings, internet!'?"

"Nah."

"Greetings, earthlings?"

"Maybe."

"Forget about it!" Lisa yelled from her office. "They all stink. Just start with your second sentence." Lisa scooted her office chair to the door and leaned out.

"When did you get a copy, Lisa? I only sent it to Sam."

"I'm copied on everything. It's something I learned from Sid Boffin. And I hear everything in the office, so keep your yapping down. As far as your blog post goes, it's OK. It's not as bad as some of Sam's early crap."

"Uh, thanks, Lisa," Ron said.

"Yeah, thanks," Sam added.

"Don't mention it. Get back to work." Lisa rolled her chair back into her office.

Sotto voce to Ron, Sam said, "Lisa actually likes your post. You kind of have to interpret her words."

* * *

"I can't believe we're going to the White House again!" Sam exclaimed as they drove to the Peoria airport on Halloween morning.

"Even I'm excited, an old, jaded newspaper editor," Lisa added.

"You're not old!"

"But I am jaded."

"Are you jaded of me?"

"No." She smiled.

"Then you're not jaded."

"I love you, Sam."

"I still melt when you say that."

"That's why I love you."

"I wonder how the Trumps will be different from the Obamas? I mean, I've read about them, but people are always different than what you read about them in the news."

"Not our *Midley Beacon* news!" Lisa said, sitting up straight.

"Of course not!"

"We'll just have to give an accurate report, like we did with the Obamas."

"We were criticized for being Obama sympathizers, you know."

"Of course. That's the nature of the news business. If you're not criticized, you're not reporting accurately. People will criticize us for having dinner with the Trumps."

"We've already had several thousand cancellations."

Lisa sniffed. "And we had cancellations after we ate with the Obamas. I had Don do some data mining on those: most of them resubscribed to the website within a couple of months. I expect the same with any other cancellations. The *Midley Beacon* is where the world goes for zombie news."

"After all, we *are* zombies."

Sam and Lisa arrived at the airport and met Dan Cosana. Lisa hired him full time to fly the *Midley Beacon*'s new private jet. She said it cost less to pay him a full salary and benefits than it had to pay him part time, on call. They'd also hired a copilot, June Livermore. She had worked for the airlines but left to rear her two children. She had been delighted to fly again, based in her hometown of Peoria. Her husband, Walt, quit his job as a project manager to write novels and stays at home with the children.

They climbed on board and flew the short trip to Gary, Indiana, to pick up George and Diane, who were also invited to the White House for recognition and dinner.

Diane and George awaited them at the private aviation concourse at the Gary airport. They took the stairs up to the aircraft cabin.

"Hi, Lisa!" Diane called from the stairs.

Dan Cosana and June Livermore greeted the couple. "Welcome to the *Midley One*."

"Oh, you're new!" Diane exclaimed. "Thanks for joining us! I'm Diane!" She vigorously pumped June's hand.

"Ease up, Diane. She's gotta fly the plane," Lisa urged.

"Of course! Sorry. I get carried away, sometimes."

"Have a seat in our lounge, George and Diane. We now have a flight attendant to serve us food. I held off eating until you got here. This is Dustin Fowler."

"Hi. What can I serve you folks? Here's today's menu: smoked salmon on toast, with cream cheese and capers; french onion soup; or potato and leek soup."

"Yes," Sam said.

"One of each?" Dustin said.

"Yes."

"I'll have the same," George said.

"And me too!" Diane chimed in.

"OK, I might as well go along with you pigs," Lisa said.

"We're zombie human beings, not pigs!" Diane said. "Young man, in case you didn't know, zombies eat about twice as much as other human beings. This is my second breakfast."

"Like hobbits," George murmured.

"Beverages?" Dustin asked. "We've got coffee, tea, soda, and a complete bar."

"Coffee," George said.

"Tea," Diane added.

"Hmmm. I'd like a beer," Sam said.

Looking at her watch, Lisa said, "Yeah, it's lunchtime. It's not too early for a cocktail. I'll have a dry martini."

"You hard-drinking newspaper people will corrupt us church people!" Diane laughed.

"Hey! I go to church too!" Sam protested.

"And sometimes, even I do," Lisa added. "I do get a chuckle out of fulfilling the old cliché of booze-at-lunch-type editor. Although I regret to say, alcohol doesn't have quite the effect it did in my non-zombie days."

"Really? I wouldn't have thought that," Dustin said as he mixed her martini.

"It's quite true. The ECHZ bacteria treat alcohol as a poison to be overcome, and we zombies metabolize it at more than twice the normal rate," Diane commented.

"I can see I'm going to learn a lot about zombies in this job. This is my first flight."

"So we can say, 'Welcome aboard' to you!" Sam said. "How'd you get with 'Zombie Airlines'? Lisa hired you, I know."

"I'm working my way through culinary school and needed some money. Making food and serving it is right up my alley."

"I didn't want to hire any of the traditional flight attendants," Lisa said. "I was looking for someone who could make some good food, more than anyone with airline experience."

"And that was me!"

Arriving in Washington, DC, at the Ronald Reagan Washington National Airport, a couple of hours later, the two couples were met by the presidential limousine, complete with Secret Service agents. One was their old friend Agent Smith. They had met him when he and his fellow agents saved President Obama and his family from zombie turkeys on that Thanksgiving in 2015.

He still wore dark sunglasses, and his musculature still made his dark suit bulge. The scar on his face from the zombie turkeys he had fought was gone though.

"Hi, Agent Smith! You're looking good these days."

"Thank you, Sam," he answered in his low, soft voice. "I can thank Diane and George and SPEwZ for that."

"You mean, you've taken the zombie blood cure?" Diane asked.

"Yes. That was the only way I could get reinstated in the Secret Service after I lost my eye." He took off his dark glasses. Two brilliant-blue eyes looked at them. He quickly put his glasses back on.

"Do you have contact lenses?" George asked.

"Yes. For security, it's important that people see me as a normal person, without suspecting my zombie blood. They also help with shielding me from too much daylight."

"I feel better knowing we have a zombie protecting us," Diane said.

"And I feel better knowing you're all zombies, able to handle yourselves in a firefight. I saw the video of your fight on the *Rule Britannia.* Well done."

Sam felt he had been given a Medal of Honor.

"You do have your White House security badges that were sent to you? Please let me see them."

They each showed their badges—except for Sam. "I don't know where mine is!"

"You won't be able to enter without them."

"Here's yours, Sam." Lisa pulled it from her purse. "I knew you'd forget it."

Agent Smith and another agent drove the limo, while the two couples rode in the back.

Lisa said, "Look! A wet bar!"

"I don't drink," Diane said.

"You just said you don't get much thrill from alcohol anymore," George commented.

"Right. I also said I like fulfilling clichés, like drinking in a limo. Here's to zombie life!" Lisa hoisted a Manhattan in a toast.

"Hear, hear!" Sam said, lifting a bottle of beer.

"To life, L'chaim," George murmured as he sipped a pinot grigio.

"Can I toast with ginger ale?" Diane asked.

"Of course!" Lisa said.

"Over the lips and through the gums, look out, stomach— here it comes!" she said, taking a gulp.

The limo dropped them off at the south portico of the White House. The agents escorted them up the steps to the first-floor entrance.

Melania Trump greeted them from the porch. "Welcome to the White House! I'm so glad to finally meet you, after reading all about you in the *Midley Beacon*!"

"Nice to meet you, Mrs. Trump," Sam said.

"Just call me Melania, please. I'll take you to the Oval Office, where you'll meet Donald. After the ceremony, I'll take you on a tour of the White House."

Agent Smith followed quietly behind the two couples and Mrs. Trump.

"Ceremony? What ceremony?" Lisa asked. "I know we were invited here for some recognition for fighting zombies and a dinner, but I didn't know about a ceremony."

"I would have come just for the dinner," Sam murmured.

"Oh, that's Donald's little surprise for you. It's not too long. You should be done in an hour or so."

"I get nervous when the president has a surprise for me," Diane said.

"I can't imagine you ever being nervous," George said.

"It is true that President Obama surprised us on the Oprah show," Lisa admitted.

"And that wasn't bad at all."

"I'm sure Donald's surprise will be better than that," Melania said.

They entered the famed Oval Office, and President Trump smiled and rose to shake their hands. "Diane! George! Sam!

Lisa! It's great to see you! Thanks for coming. You guys worked hard. Trust me on this. You're hard workers. Come with me to the South Lawn. I've got a huge surprise for you!"

President and Mrs. Trump led them to the South Lawn, where to their surprise, news crews were waiting with cameras.

"Hi, everyone!" the president called. "Are you ready to go?" he asked the camera crew.

They nodded. "Yes, Mr. President."

"Great. Sam, Lisa, George, Diane, here's the press crew." He gestured to a group of twenty people seated on chairs on the lawn. "They're a great bunch, most of the time," he said with a chuckle.

There was a row of four chairs behind the presidential podium and another group of chairs directly in front of the podium. The president and his wife led them to the front row of chairs, in front of the press.

The president and Melania made ready to depart, and Lisa whispered urgently, "What's this all about, Mr. President?"

"Oh, you'll find out in a minute or two. We'll be right back." He and Melania walked away.

"I hate not knowing what's going on!" Lisa whispered to Sam.

"Sssh! They're starting!"

An attractive lady stepped to the podium

"Ladies and gentlemen, the recipients of the Presidential Medal of Freedom.

"Lisa Jane Melvin."

Wide-eyed, Lisa rose and walked to the first chair behind the podium, to a shower of applause from the assembled press.

"Sam Alfred Melvin."

Looking like a stunned ox, Sam followed Lisa.

"Diane Elizabeth Newby."

Smiling from ear to ear, Diane almost danced up the stairs to the stage.

"George Allen Newby."

George stoically followed his wife to the platform, with his blankest face hiding his inner shock.

A fanfare played.

"Ladies and gentlemen, the president of the United States and Mrs. Melania Trump."

The audience arose, applauding as the band played "Hail to the Chief."

The president took his position behind the podium and spoke. "It's great to be here today to recognize four outstanding Americans, two American couples. All four are part of a newly recognized minority group, zombies.

"Lisa Melvin began the *Midley Beacon* newspaper eighteen years ago, one of the first to offer content online. Then three years ago, she risked life and limb in reporting on the zombie turkey apocalypse, which catapulted her and the *Midley Beacon* into national prominence.

"Not content to rest on her laurels, she built the paper's small business by specializing in zombie news. She and the *Midley Beacon* were so successful, she attracted the attention of the international criminal Sid Boffin, who sought to kill her and take over the hub of zombie news media.

"He nearly succeeded. After a near-death experience, Lisa was saved by the zombie blood treatment. She worked closely with US intelligence agencies and participated in the final assault on his yacht, removing him permanently from our nation's terrorist threat list.

"Through it all, Lisa Melvin displayed courage, initiative, patriotism, and good old-fashioned American grit. She epitomizes American entrepreneurship and sacrifices for one's country. Lisa Melvin, I present to you the Presidential Medal of Freedom." The president placed the medal over Lisa's head and shook her hand.

"Sam Alfred Melvin worked with Lisa at the *Midley Beacon* before and during the turkey apocalypse. He was the point man in the assault on the turkey threat and risked his life even more than Lisa did. Once the *Midley Beacon* focused on zombie news, he was the first one on the scene in zombie animal and zombie human news.

"He too was caught in the Midley inferno when Sid Boffin blew up a gasoline tanker and barely escaped with his life through zombie blood. He too shared his zombie knowledge and insights with our intelligence community as they tracked Sid Boffin down to his yacht. He rode a zombie bull into battle and received severe injuries while fighting alongside US Marines.

"Sam never wavered in his courage, his commitment to the American cause, in freeing America from this cyborg-manipulating terrorist. Sam Melvin, I present to you the Presidential Medal of Freedom." The president awarded Sam his medal and shook his hand. Sam sat down, next to Lisa.

"Diane Elizabeth Newby did not intend to become a zombie, but through circumstances beyond her control contracted the zombie bacteria two years ago. She used her zombie strength and energy to subdue wild zombie animals and fight for human zombie rights. Diane created the Society for the People Equality with Zombies, which has fought tirelessly for human and zombie equality. Recently, the US Congress passed the Zombie Equality Act, which bans all discrimination based upon zombiism.

"Diane also became the spokeswomen and leader of SPEwZ Inc., the corporate arm of the SPEwZ charitable foundation. SPEwZ Inc. bought and sold zombie blood well below market value, which has led to the worldwide medical revolution and cures for amputation, blindness, deafness, Alzheimer's, and many, many other formerly incurable diseases.

"Diane would merit the Presidential Medal of Freedom for these activities alone, but she's done much more. SPEwZ Inc., built in downtown Gary, Indiana, revitalized an inner-city area. Diane participated in the final assault on Sid Boffin's Gulf of Mexico retreat, as well as in assaults in Manhattan, Kansas, and Loch Lomond, Scotland. Many times she faced death, but never as much as when the entire SPEwZ complex was destroyed in a dastardly terrorist attack.

"Diane Newby exemplifies the 'never quit' attitude of all Americans, which led to the eventual victory over the evil criminal empire. Diane Newby, I award you the Presidential Medal of Freedom." President Trump lifted the medal over her head and shook her hand. Diane shook back vigorously, smiling all the while.

Surreptitiously flexing his hand, the president called, "George Allen Newby."

George stood up.

"George Newby is the SPEwZ financial and organizational wizard. He created the nonprofit organization and incorporated SPEwZ Inc. to fund the nonprofit and other zombie charitable works.

"George fought twice in Manhattan, Kansas, and in Loch Lomond on behalf of US citizens, alongside the US military. He has risked his life dozens of times, incurring life-threatening injuries while fighting against this criminal terrorist organization. He also fought in the final battle in the Gulf of Mexico, defeating these international criminals. George Newby, I award you the Presidential Medal of Freedom." President Trump shook George's hand after settling the medal around his neck. Although the president was taller, he still looked small next to George's bulk.

"I have some important closing remarks," the president said after the two couples sat down behind him. "Just this morning Congress has issued a letter of marque commissioning the *Rule Britannia* as a privateer working as an auxiliary to the US Navy to fight other international criminals like Sid Boffin.

"I signed this marque this morning, and I have issued a commission to you two couples, Sam and Lisa Melvin and Diane and George Newby, to lead and captain this ship under my direct authorization. You will continue to work closely with our military and NSA intelligence, as you have in the past. They have several leads for you to pursue right now."

Gasping, Diane Newby exclaimed, "Zombie pirates! We're now zombie pirates!"

Overhearing her, President Trump chuckled and said, "Yes, you're the first zombie pirates in history. You've already proven your patriotism and loyalty to our nation. I can't think of anyone I'd rather lead this effort than you four."

Stunned into silence, the four stood to applause, as the TV broadcast and the live streaming ended and the press and audience departed.

"It's been great! But I've got some other appointments. I'll see you at suppertime," the president said.

After bidding the president good-bye, the two couples went on a tour of the White House with Melania. Later, after supper and after bowling in the White House bowling alley with the Trumps, they watched the classic zombie movie *Night of the Living Dead* in the White House movie room.

"It's so appropriate for Halloween!" Diane said.

"And for our zombie heroes!" the president added.

"The movie really reinforces negative stereotypes of zombies," Diane said. "But I still enjoy it. I realize how far we've come as a nation!"

"Of course, there were no real zombies to be stereotyped when the movie was made," President Trump said.

"True, but once we came on the scene, the bad images had to be overcome."

"Which you've truly done, to a huge, *huge* extent."

"I'll toast to that!" Diane raised her glass of apple cider, George and Sam their beers, Lisa her cocktail.

"To the zombie pirates!" President Trump said.

"To the United States, home of the free and the brave—and zombies!" Diane said.

Epilogue

The brilliant Mediterranean sun shone upon the azure bay around the Greek island of Kristos. Small fishing boats dotted the bay, leaving the docks and going out for the evening's fishing. From the bay, the island rose swiftly to cliffs surrounding and protecting it from fierce winter storms. Atop the highest cliff stood a white villa. Hundreds of years old, it had seen Napoleon, Mussolini, and Hitler come and go as rulers of the Mediterranean.

Inside the villa's courtyard, shaded from the sun under a striped awning, a man studied a screen covering the wall. The screen showed a large ship with helicopters hovering over it. Puffs of smoke came from the ship, and two of the helicopters crashed into the sea.

Gesturing with his hand, the screen zoomed in on the stern of the ship. It showed a bloody battle scene between uniformed military men and hula girls, of all things. Zooming in still more, the camera followed the military unit into the transom dock, where a large powerboat was docked. A smaller sailing yacht lodged in front of it. Beyond both of these ships, the camera proceeded into a submarine dock. The fighters swarmed over the two-person sub docked there and then left, seemingly surprised and disappointed.

He flicked his fingers in a series of complicated gestures, and the screen's scene suddenly changed. Now it showed the back of a man's head, a submarine control panel, and a view portal. On the control panel were, of all things, two chipmunks.

The man quietly watched the progress of the sub as it dove and leveled off. Then, unexpectedly, it dove again. The man frantically pushed some controls. The scene went black.

Annoyed, the man snapped the fingers of his left hand. The scene reappeared, fuzzy, in black and white, as normal for the hidden infrared camera. The sub's pilot, glowing white, crawled under the control panel. Some muffled cursing reached his ear. Then the lights appeared in the sub again.

The dark-haired submarine pilot took his chair again. The sub climbed steeply. Without looking, he whipped out a pistol from his shoulder holster and snapped off a shot. He placed the gun on the panel as he continued to climb.

From the camera's perspective, the man in the villa could see a chipmunk climbing up the control panel carefully out of the pilot's sight and seemingly tiptoeing toward the gun. Once there, it seemed to grasp the trigger with its two little paws. Instantly, the submariner snatched the gun, and it went off. A jet of water shot from the broken portal. Savagely, the chipmunk was crushed in the man's bare hand.

The pilot jerked the submarine's control yoke back, and it went straight up. The glow of daylight could be seen on the distant surface. Then the already leaking viewport shattered. The man on the submarine barely escaped as tons of water filled the sub. He cowered beneath the control panel. The lights went out again.

The watcher snapped his fingers again, and the scene changed to black and white once more. A glowing white human form under the control panel was the only illumination. Its glow slowly dimmed as the cold water sucked the heat—and life from him.

A sudden spasm took the man, and then he was still. The man in the villa watched the form as the light from the body heat slowly faded to blackness. That meant the man was the same temperature as the water.

"Damn it." Startled by his own swearing, John Smith went back through his flawless memory to when he'd last sworn. Ten, twenty, twenty-four years ago when Kim Il-sung had died and he had serious trouble getting the next Korean despot, Kim Jong-Un, under his control. He'd said "damn it" then too.

Now he'd lost his best agent, his key clone. His hierarchical control structure of his financial criminal empire required subordinates he could completely trust. Who better than a clone of himself? They all thought he was their father. They came to him for advice and help when in trouble. The latter rarely happened. They were as smart as he was.

In fact, that was what went wrong. Vik was in trouble and didn't think of asking for his help. John Smith saw several things he could have done to save Vik.

Now he had to clean up after Vik's mess. First, he would contact his other clones around the world and review Vik's defeat and how he could have helped him if he had asked. This would subtly remind them to ask for help. All of them knew there were at least one other brother or sister of theirs in his empire. It was best to keep his network in cells, so any one failure would be contained. He also didn't want any future failures in dealing with the zombies.

John set up the ninety-three conference calls, one for each clone. Each of his sons and daughters had a virtual reality conference room where they could meet with him—"Papa Smith," as they knew him—or each other, or their subordinates. It was faster and prevented dangerous travel, which exposed them to detection.

The calls would take over a hundred hours, but neither he nor his clones needed to sleep anymore. That was one technical advance his Chinese clone, Wang Li, had developed. He kept the technology secret to retain an edge for his family.

Through genetic manipulation, John Smith adjusted his clones to each of the major races. At this point in his career, he genetically engineered his children as easily as he changed his race and appearance through genetically induced skin changes. Occasionally, he lost track of which race he had been originally. He smiled as he reviewed his history for perhaps a second.

The calls took the next five days. John Smith also took advantage of these conferences to maneuver several of his clones into taking over remnants of Vik's empire. That was an easy task since they were all as ambitious as he was. He liked getting multiple things done at once.

After they had all been warned and learned Vik's lessons in dealing with the zombie threat, then he'd take direct action against the zombies. Finally SPEwZ and the pesky *Midley Beacon* would be out of his hair.

He ran his hand through the slick salt-and-pepper pompadour he favored. It made him look like a fop, a look he accentuated with ruffled shirts, French cuffs, scented pomade, and handkerchiefs inside his cuffs. Being thought a fop made everyone, even his clones, underestimate him. He knew half of his clones were considering how to take his place, and he assumed the other half were also thinking about it but were better at hiding it. None had come close to overthrowing him. Typically, he'd maneuver them to attack another crime boss, defeat him or her, and think they were on top of his empire.

He'd been in charge of his empire for over a hundred years, beginning before he'd changed his name to John Smith, forever obliterating any trail to his past. He looked forward to his next hundred years of world domination. Once he cleared the world of zombies.

The End

Chapter 1 - Somalia

Dirac sighed with relief when the US flag came down and the surrender flag went up on the mast of the titanic luxury yacht. He didn't mind firing rounds from his AK-47 over their heads, but he hated killing people. He knew they were only infidels, but they were still people.

Inhaling the salted breeze, he grinned back at Muhammed. He cheered and laughed in his seat behind the M2 machine gun in the bow of the boat they used to patrol the coasts and fishing waters of Somalia. The sun gleamed off his white teeth.

"Look, Dirac!" he said. "They're stopping!"

True enough. The bow wave ceased as he watched. A pod of dolphins ended their sporting on the wave and submerged. The gleaming white yacht loomed above them. What were they doing in the fishing waters of Somalia? He couldn't imagine the wealth on board. Enough for their whole village to eat well for a year!

Their supreme leader, Omar Ogala, organized Somali fishermen and former coast guard sailors to patrol their fishing waters. He ordered them to capture any fishing or cargo vessels they spotted. He told them the Americans and Europeans no longer cared about Somalia with the other crises around the world and they could defend their coasts from foreign competition—and dumpers. Many foreign nations, knowing Somalia's military weakness, sent cargo ships full of pollutants and dumped them into their waters.

Dirac never expected to see a luxury ship here. It was as big as a cruise liner, but apparently a private yacht. He'd seen one once before when an Arab sheik visited Mogadishu. This one was three times the size! The owner would pay big to get it back. Maybe even a billion dollars? He couldn't imagine that much money, and he was good with numbers. Let's see: fourteen million people lived in Somalia. Divide a billion dollars among them would give each about seventy dollars. Unbelievable. A family of five could live comfortably for a year on that!

He came along as a navigator, fighter, and boarder, guiding their boat along the shore of Somalia and into the Arabian Gulf for several days, before leading them back. Besides Muhammed and him, there was Zahi, another fighter and boarder, and Ali, their captain.

"Dirac," Ali said, "you and Zahi board this ship and take the helm. You will follow us back to Hobyo. Muhammed and I will stay on the boat and keep the machine gun on them."

"Yes, sir," he said.

Ali took the megaphone they carried for ship-to-ship communication. "Let us board! Let us board! Or we will gun your ship!"

Dirac didn't understand English, of course, but he knew what Ali was saying. Ali was the only one who knew any English.

"Don't shoot! Give us time! We have to get our ladder!" Surprisingly, the person spoke in Arabic. Good Arabic too, but with a strange Saudi and European accent. More surprisingly, it was a woman, a blonde, from what he could see of the figure leaning over the railing far above us. He kept a close watch on her. Strictly for security purposes, of course.

They kept their boat about fifty meters away from the ship and watched the crew scurry about the many decks. Dirac counted five including the main deck, and there were at least three more decks below the main one.

Finally a rope ladder unrolled from the main deck, perhaps ten meters above them. They came close to the ship. A pod of dolphins flashed under their boat. Then they leapt out of the water and into it.

Only, they weren't the dolphins he had seen earlier. Four people in green wet suits landed with heavy thumps in Dirac's boat. They had no breathing equipment, not even snorkels. They took off their goggles, and their eyes shone bright red in the sun.

"Zombies!" Ali cried. "Shoot them!"

Automatically Dirac sprayed the nearest with his AK-47. He heard the others fire too. Muhammed shot the largest one with the big .50-caliber machine gun. That could cut a man in two.

Dozens of red craters appeared in the green wet suit of the one Dirac shot. But she—a white, brown-haired woman—didn't go down. Her brows furrowed in anger, and shouting in English, she ripped the gun from his hand and threw it into the ocean. He was like a baby with a rattle taken by his parent. The other zombies did the same, except the big one. He grabbed the barrel of the machine gun in both hands and wrenched it from Muhammed. Dirac could hear the zombie's flesh sizzle on the hot barrel. Then the big zombie bent the barrel into a right angle. Rubbing his hands together afterward, the burned skin fell on the deck of their boat. Pink skin showed on his palms.

He was enormous, bigger than two Somalis put together. His red eyes looked out of his calm, square face. The bullets from the machine gun had sliced the wet suit open across his chest, and more pink skin showed in the gap. As he watched, brown hair grew.

The fighters were all struck dumb with shock and terror. Then the woman Dirac had shot called up to the blond woman on the main deck. She yelled down in Arabic, "All of you, lie down on the deck, and you will live."

They quickly obeyed.

Dirac heard a splash. Apparently, she'd dived into the water. She then leapt from the water and landed in their boat.

"I will direct you, and you will listen and obey," said a tall, shapely blond woman with bright-red eyes. She asked each of their names and roles and plans for taking the yacht. She

184

consulted briefly in English with the others. "Very well, we will follow through with your plans. Dirac and Zahi will come on board with us. Ali and Muhammed will stay in the boat, and we'll all go to Hobyo."

Numbly, Dirac climbed the rope ladder to the deck, following Zahi. He tried to process all he had learned in the few minutes of their aborted attack. *They hijacked us. But they're zombies! They want to follow our plan. But they're zombies! We're going to Hobyo. But they're zombies! What will happen there? But they're zombies!*

Paranormal Privateers will be available for sale on Amazon in May 2018. Check my blog andyzach.net for the latest news.

Andy Zach

Author Bio

Photo by Barb Lloyd

Andy Zach was born Anastasius Zacharias, in Greece. His parents were both zombies. Growing up, he loved animals of all kinds. After moving to the United States as a child, in high school he won a science fair by bringing toads back from suspended animation. Before turning to fiction, Andy published his PhD thesis "Methods of Revivification for Various Species of the Kingdom Animalia" in the prestigious JAPM, *Journal of Paranormal Medicine.* Andy, in addition to being the foremost expert on paranormal animals, enjoys breeding phoenixes. He lives in Illinois with his five phoenixes.

QUICK ORDER FORM

Satisfaction Guaranteed

⌨ Web site orders: andyzach.net
⌨ jms61614-andyzach@yahoo.com
🖥 **Postal orders:**   Zombie Turkey Orders
                              PO Box 10705
                              Peoria, Illinois 61614

Please send the following Books

I understand that I may return any of them for a full refund—for any reason, no questions asked.

See our website for FREE information on:
Contests, giveaways, other books, speaking/interviews, mailing lists, fan discussion forums

Name:

Address:

City, State/Province, Postal Code

Tel:

Email:

Sales tax:

Shipping by air:

Payment: Cheque; credit card

Visa, MasterCard, Optima, AMEX, Discover
Card number:
Name on card:
Exp. date: /

Made in the USA
Coppell, TX
29 November 2019